HEINEMANN NEW WINDMILLS

YOUR FRIEND, REBECCA

At the beginning of this story Rebecca isn't anybody's friend. At school all the teachers seem to pick on her and the only boy she is interested in hardly knows she exists. Since her mother died Rebecca and her father have barely managed to talk to each other.

It takes the acting out of the tragedy of King Lear in Miss Gloucester's Drama Workshop to make Rebecca see just what the loss of her mother has meant to her father and come to terms with his unhappiness, as well as her own.

ABOUT THE AUTHOR

Linda Hoy lives in Sheffield with her three teenage children. She taught English in a local comprehensive school for nine years, before leaving in order to devote more energy to writing and working for the peace campaign. As a Quaker she is also deeply involved with work for young people.

YOUR FRIEND, REBECCA

LINDA HOY

HEINEMANN
NEW WINDMILLS

Heinemann Educational
a division of Heinemann Educational Books Ltd
Halley Court
Jordan Hill
Oxford OX2 8EJ
OXFORD LONDON EDINBURGH
MADRID ATHENS BOLOGNA PARIS
MELBOURNE SYDNEY AUCKLAND SINGAPORE TOKYO
IBADAN NAIROBI HARARE GABARONE
PORTSMOUTH NH (USA)

First published in 1981 by The Bodley Head Ltd, London.

First published in the New Windmill Series 1992

93 94 95 10 9 8 7 6 5 4 3 2

British Cataloguing in Publication Data
for this title is available from the British Library

ISBN 0 435 12388 2

Printed by Clays Ltd, St Ives plc

YOUR FRIEND, REBECCA

LINDA HOY

HEINEMANN
NEW WINDMILLS

Heinemann Educational
a division of Heinemann Educational Books Ltd
Halley Court
Jordan Hill
Oxford OX2 8EJ
OXFORD LONDON EDINBURGH
MADRID ATHENS BOLOGNA PARIS
MELBOURNE SYDNEY AUCKLAND SINGAPORE TOKYO
IBADAN NAIROBI HARARE GABARONE
PORTSMOUTH NH (USA)

First published in 1981 by The Bodley Head Ltd, London.

First published in the New Windmill Series 1992

93 94 95 10 9 8 7 6 5 4 3 2

British Cataloguing in Publication Data
for this title is available from the British Library

ISBN 0 435 12388 2

Printed by Clays Ltd, St Ives plc

1

'I will do such things,
What they are, yet I know not, but they shall be
The terrors of the earth.'

(Lear, *King Lear*, Act II, Scene IV)

'Which part are you auditioning for, dear?'

Miss Hoggit leered down at me and her false teeth rattled like dried-up snails in a treacle tin.

It wasn't just calling me *dear* – it was the way she said it. It made you feel as proud of yourself as a four-year-old kid who's just been and wet her knickers in the Wendy House. I don't like her. We call her The Hog when she's not around.

'Erm . . . er . . .' I shuffled about like an idiot. I didn't know what to say. You see, the truth of it was that I didn't know any Shakespeare and so I'd got no idea what parts there were. All I knew was that the play was called *King Lear* and Darren Edmunds was going to be in it. He was this lad that I fancied in the fifth year. They knew all about *King Lear* because they were doing it for O Level. I couldn't tell it from *The Sound of Music* myself. I wouldn't have minded just being a lady-in-waiting or the back legs of a horse or something. I didn't know what to say.

'You *have* put your name down for the audition . . .' she said, tapping her fancy Papermate on her notebook. Pigs don't smile for very long.

'Yes . . .' I started, shuffling about again like a remedial clog dancer. At this rate I'd probably finish up as something completely ridiculous like second-fairy's-tea-masher's-helper or substitute-prompter's-wardrobe-assistant. I knew I was useless but I still wanted a proper part.

'Well?'

I had to say something. I swallowed hard and took a deep breath. 'King Lear,' I said.

I could actually hear The Hog gasping slightly and her eyebrows shot upwards. There was a painful silence. Well, if it was called *King Lear*, then he was bound to be in it somewhere, wasn't he? And I couldn't think of any other parts they might have.

I saw her eyes looking me up and down and taking in my straggling brown hair and size eighty-eight bust (centimetres that is, not inches). She was thinking how I'd pass for an old man easily with a false beard, a walking stick, a face mask and a body transplant – if I just mimed, that is, and somebody else did the voice.

All of a sudden she looked up at me and tried to smile. Her face looked as though it was going to crack in half any minute with the strain. 'All right then, dear,' she snorted. 'We've got no one else for Lear as yet. I'll put your name down.'

Walking out of school, late. It's five o'clock, March. Cold and misty.

You walk along, entombed in a cavern of gloom. You're invisible. Nobody else can see you. And there's a kind of stillness round about with swirling shapes and soft pattering sounds, and you're all there is. Isolated. Blind. You don't have to smile and say hello to people because you can't see them.

And of course I know I've made a mess of the audition. Well, I'm just one big mess from start to finish anyway. But there's nobody to talk to about it, you see. Not at the moment. And that seems to matter more than anything else just now. So what I keep doing, I keep talking to myself as I'm walking down this street. Talking out loud because I get the feeling that this mist is thick around me like a padded cell, keeping listeners out. 'There's nobody to care about it,' I say. Like an idiot. 'I've made a mess of the audition and nobody's bothered. Nobody cares about me. Nobody cares about me. Nobody . . .' The idea is that if I keep saying these things to myself often enough, I'll get used to the idea. I'm trying to brainwash myself, you see, so I don't get upset about it any more. But of course it doesn't work. Perhaps I'm just too sorry for myself. I start to cry like I always do. Fat, blubbering tears. Wiping my nose on my hand because no one can see me.

A passing poodle stops and glares at me as if I'm a refugee from a lunatic asylum. And I think that if it was always misty you could walk down the street crying every day and nobody would ever know.

Like I said before, I'm a bit of a mess.

The house is empty and freezing cold; even the breakfast things aren't washed up yet and it's Crispy Cod Fries for tea. I take them out of the top of the fridge, open the packet and find that they're all welded together like frozen cannon-balls. I stand them in a pyramid in the frying-pan and kid myself that they'll thaw out whilst I'm doing the washing-up.

They're just fish balls really instead of fish fingers, but if you want to know why they don't call them fish balls, well there was this little kid in the supermarket whose mum was just buying some fish fingers and he said, 'Mum, I didn't know that fish had fingers . . .', and if you see how that would work with the fish balls, then you'll understand why they gave them an idiotic name like Crispy Cod Fries instead.

I try to chisel a couple of them apart with a potato peeler but the blade just bends a bit, so I try bashing it with the tea caddy for extra weight (we did Levers last year in Science). A cod ball whizzes round the kitchen like a supersonic doughnut and splashes down into the cat's breakfast. I think about fishing it out and rinsing it under the tap, and then making sure *he* gets that one when it's cooked, but I decide against it. The chances are that it'd only finish up on my plate anyway. I'm unlucky like that. I decide to wipe the spilled tea leaves out of the frying-pan instead. Like I said before, I'm a bit of a mess.

I switch the cooker full on to start the cannon-balls defrosting and put the kettle on for the washing-up. I've still got my coat on. The kitchen is as warm as a Polar Bear's tombstone in a blizzard. I put the cornflakes and the marmalade back into the cupboard and shake the tablecloth. Then I turn it over and put it back on the table. I plonk the butter dish on the place where I spilled my coffee last night and the sugar bowl over the place where I burnt a hole with the frying-pan.

Of course it wasn't like this when Mum was here. The kitchen was always warm then because she was in here baking with the oven on, and when you came home from school there'd be the smell of fresh-baked bread. Or sponge cakes. Or scones . . . or home-made jam . . . or that delicious pineapple upside-down pudding with glacé cherries in the middle of the pineapple rings and a little touch of cinammon . . . I try not to think about things like that too often, but sometimes I think that's what I miss most of all about my mother. I don't just miss the food – I'm not so greedy. But coming home from school, especially in the winter-time, and the house being warm and tidy and a lovely hot meal nearly ready. I unplug the kettle and fill up the washing-up bowl with hot water and wish I'd remembered to buy some washing-up liquid on Saturday.

Then there's a smell of burning. I look up at the cooker and see black smoke waving at me from the frying-pan. The fish balls at the bottom are burning round the edges, whilst the ones on top are still welded together with ice. In Cookery we do ludicrous things like peeling chilled cucumbers and chopping crusts off sandwiches. They think even a retarded pig-swill masher would know how to fry fish balls.

I find the fish slice and try to chisel the burnt fish balls off the bottom of the pan but they fall to pieces instead. The burnt batter stays stuck to the bottom of the frying-pan and the square slab of raw fish from the inside hops away to smoulder in some spot of its own. I never was one for *cordon bleu*. I turn the ring down to number two and carry on washing up the breakfast things.

The kitchen always used to be neat and tidy. And all the shelves stacked high with food. Not tinned beans and packets of dehydrated trifle and synthetic cheesecake like most people have, but all home-made. Every September we used to go blackberry picking, and then we'd have a whole shelf full of jam jars with neat little white labels bordered in blue and the date and BLACKBERRY JAM printed on them in black felt pen. She'd make lemon curd as well when the lemons and eggs were cheap in the market, and it was delicious. All thick and tangy. Then there were the pickles and the chutney made with home-grown vegetables. She used to like gardening. All in rows in the pantry, labelled, dated. All of them delicious and good for you. That was what my mother was like. She's dead now.

Later on I have my tea and leave his in the oven on a plate. It'll get dry and shrivelled up, but he won't say anything. It serves him right. I usually make the tea early because sometimes he comes straight home from work and we sit down together, staring at each other. Not knowing what to say. But most days, like now, he's late and I have my tea first. When he comes in then I'm watching the television or pretending to do some homework upstairs, and then we don't have to talk to each other at all. I think we like it best that way.

After tea I watch the television, not that there's anything

on that I'm interested in. There never is. I have a look at my homework first, which is learning a list of words in French. I just glance at them and kid myself that I'll learn them properly later on. I won't, of course. I never do.

So I glance down the list and the one thing I notice straightaway about these words is that nearly all of them are completely useless. Like 'the king' for instance and 'the battle'. As far as I can remember, France hasn't even got a king and I bet you could walk around in Paris all day long without ever having to talk about 'the battle'. They're not the sort of words you need for everyday conversations. 'The eyes' – that might come in handy, but not 'blind (adj.)'. Not unless you were blind, of course, and wanted to tell everybody, but then you wouldn't be able to read the list in the first place, would you?

Perhaps it might have been useful for King Harold when William the Conqueror came over and said, 'Let's have a battle.' Harold could have thought he was saying, 'Let's bomb off down to Marks and Spencer's and get the lads some Y-fronts,' if he hadn't bothered to do his French homework. Perhaps that's why he lost. Anyway, there's no battle on for me. Not at the moment.

So, even though I haven't got anything else to do all evening, I still don't learn my French vocab. I watch the television like I always do and it's completely boring and futile like it always is, but I get so I can't even be bothered standing up to switch the set off. That's how I am nowadays. Useless. He's had his tea and gone out. We hardly talk to each other but, like I said, I think we like it best that way.

2

'O! let me not be mad, not mad, sweet heaven;
Keep me in temper; I would not be mad!'

(Lear, Act I, Scene V)

'Put your names at the top of the papers and number down from one to twenty.'

She has this horrible cackling laugh, Miss Runt, which she puts on specially when she's doing something foul like giving you a test or telling you you've got a detention. She'd make a very good prison warder I think because she'd get a real kick out of telling people they were being put in five weeks' solitary confinement. She'd giggle whilst she was telling them, cackling happily away like a witch. Or one of those women who work at the dentist's and shove you into the room with the chair in. All manicured finger-nails and pink lipstick. They're always smiling. Except that half her teeth have fallen out. We call her Gertie.

I look across to Sarah Swille who sits next to me in French, but today she's got her paper swizzled round and her arm accidentally on purpose across it so I can't see any of her answers. I hate her. I hope she gets them all wrong.

'*Numéro un* . . .' Miss G. Runt starts off in this fantastically exaggerated French accent. If all French people talk like Gertie Runt I wouldn't go there to be buried. She talks like a circus.

'. . . the battle.' And then, as if you're stupid or deaf or something, she says it again only twice as loud and three times as ridiculous.

I looked at that one. I know it's something like battle only a bit different. I put '*La baittaille*'. It looks very French.

'Numéro deux . . .' She says it 'nooooo maaaaayy roooohhhh . . . derrrrrr!!! The king . . . the king . . .'

I look around the classroom and everybody else is madly scribbling away. All you can hear is the sound their posh expensive pens make on the paper, although if you listen very carefully, you can sometimes hear the noise of their brains working overtime as well. I'm looking for somebody to mouth me the answers, but everybody else is staring at their papers or at Gertie, waiting for *numéro* three.

'Numéro . . .'

I scribble down any old rubbish and when she sees me trying to look over Sarah Swille's shoulder, I pretend my eyes are just glazed, sort of hypnotized. Fixed. Perhaps she'll think I'm going to faint or . . .

'Keep your eyes on your own work, Rebecca,' she says sharply.

I want to cry. But of course I don't. I put down *'Les yeux'* for eyes because I've remembered that one from the lesson. I don't know why. That's one out of twenty anyway.

And so it goes on. I hate French. I think they ought to ask everybody in the first year whether they're thinking of going across to live in France or not. Those that aren't shouldn't have to learn any. I wouldn't. It makes just as much sense to me, learning French, as learning Martian. I reckon I'm just as likely to go to Mars as go to France.

'Et . . . numéro vingt . . . blind, the adjective . . . b . . . er . . . l . . . i . . . n . . . d.'

I've forgotten that one as well, and when I see her staring at me wondering why I'm not writing anything, I try to make myself look ill again so she'll think I'm going to faint or something. I'm always doing that. It never works though.

'Now, change papers, please. Boys, find a girl to change with, will you?'

I sit there staring down at my paper so none of the lads'll think I'm looking at them. All the other girls hold their papers in the air, waving them about at lads they fancy. I don't fancy any of the lads in our class. They're all foul. So I just sit there waiting, staring at the desk.

'Hurry up, *please,*' screeches Gertie. 'We'd like to have the test marked *this* week, if you don't mind.' She always says that.

All the kids rush about then, staggering back to their places, and two of the lads shout, 'Please, miss, we 'aven't changed yet.'

I look up, trying to get one of them to notice me, but neither of them do.

'Never mind,' says Gertie. 'Change with each other.' And then we start off marking the test. Everybody marking someone else's, except me, and I just hope that no one'll notice. Sarah Swille does. She gives me a superior sort of look as if I've just crawled out from under the back of a pig's trotter, and sets off marking the paper in front of her at eighty miles an hour, even before Gertie has started reading out the answers.

I look hard at my paper and listen carefully to the answers, even though the words don't bear any resemblance to the ones I've written down. Except for '*Les yeux*' that is. The eyes. I think about cheating and filling the words in as Gertie reads them out, but Sarah keeps glaring at me all the time as if she knows just what I'm thinking. I wish her face would drop off.

I try very hard not to cry because you show yourself up when you do that, but sometimes it's touch and go. I blink hard and dab my eyes with my cardi sleeve as if I'm just scraping dead earwigs out from my eyelashes.

Gertie wants to see me afterwards and I wait behind in the classroom when everybody else has gone to Maths. I don't mind missing ten minutes of Maths, actually. I hate that worse than French.

'Well?'

I don't say anything. I make sucking noises to stop myself from screaming and stare down at her feet. She's wearing a pair of those platform-soled shoes that were in fashion about twenty million years ago. I think she must have got them from a jumble sale.

'Are you chewing, Rebecca?'

'No, miss.'

'You do know there's a school rule about chewing gum, don't you? It's a disgusting habit . . .'

I want to scream again and now I can't even suck my cheeks in to stop myself. I swallow hard. She must be retarded. I've told her I'm not chewing anything and she still keeps going on about it.

'. . . and it's hardly fair on the cleaners. You wouldn't like the job of scraping old chewing-gum off the radiators, would you?'

I feel as if I could strangle her. 'No, miss,' I say, still staring at her shoes. I think she's dyed them. They look as if they were pink once and now they're an unusual shade of yellow. Very unusual. Vomit-yellow, I'd call it.

'And it ruins the floors. Only last week the school caretaker was saying he got blobs of chewing-gum stuck inside his electric floor polisher. . .'

And they're made out of this weird sort of material. I think it's worm-skin. Worms dried and then stretched. I imagine them all laid drying on a rack like snakes and lizards are . . .

'. . . and his bristles were cemented together for three hours . . .'

I listen to her rabbiting on about the chewing-gum – that I haven't got. I hate chewing-gum. And to stop myself from having hysterics, I try to work out how many dead worms it'd take to make a pair of shoes that size.

She's got very big feet you see. We did Area in Maths in the first year.

'... so at dinner-time you can come back here ... at half-past twelve ... and learn them properly. Is that understood?'

She's got round to the French test now. I'm not bothered. It'll give me something to do after dinner. 'Yes, miss.'

'Half-past twelve then.'

I think it comes to about thirty-six big worms, and eleven and a half little ones for round the edges of the soles. It depends how well their skins stretch when they're dried. I look up.

'Yes, miss.'

'Right then, off you go.'

3

''Tis the times' plague, when madmen lead the blind.'

(Gloucester, Act IV, Scene 1)

I'm having my dinner, sitting at a table on my own, when Darren Edmunds comes in. I nearly choke when I see him. He's fantastic. He picks up a tray and joins the queue for dinner. If you come at twelve o'clock there's fish 'n' chips or cheese flan or shepherd's pie (SHEP'S PIE it says on the menu), but it's ten past twelve now so there's only shep's pie left. Anyway, like I said, I nearly choke on my synthetic doughnut when I see Darren walking in. I think he's brilliant. Then I start nibbling the rest of my doughnut ever so slowly to be sure I won't have finished by the time he gets down to the end of the queue. He just might come and sit with me, you never know. There aren't many chairs left empty.

I never used to be keen on lads at all – all the ones in our year are rubbish, anyway – but how I started fancying Darren was when I first went to the Drama Workshop at the beginning of last term. Now, this might surprise you. It certainly surprised me because I've never been one for joining in any of these dinner-time activities. I think you have enough on with the lessons. But it was when I was sitting on the floor of the toilets reading this comic and Cynthia Snort came to clear us out. She's the head girl. I was livid. There was a howling blizzard outside. You know, like eighty-miles-an-hour gales and ten feet of snow or something, and these two other girls – fifth formers they were – just turned round and said to her, 'We're on our way to Drama.' So I said the same.

I set off up the corridor with my comic, looking for somewhere else warm to sneak in and have a read, when I realized Cynthia Snort was following me. I hate her. I wish her nose would drop off. And, like I said, the weather outside was so bad you'd be dying of exposure before you got down to the playground, and the Drama Workshop was in the basement next to the boiler room. I'd never been down there before, but I knew it would be warmer there than outside. So I crept downstairs and went in.

I felt a complete idiot at first because I didn't know anybody there and of course I'd never even had a go at acting. I just slunk in and stood by the wall, hoping that nobody would notice me. But this Miss Gloucester who runs it, she just came over and put me into a group with three other kids. We had ten minutes to design a trap to catch a rampaging rhinoceros in. It was a right laugh. We spent so much time giggling that the rhinoceros came and trampled us down (it was Timothy Trotter actually, with his shirt over his head, pawing the ground with his left foot and snorting). I really enjoyed it. I was sorry when we had to leave at one o'clock, and I've been going every week since. That's how I got to know Darren. The groups keep changing round, you see, and you get to know everybody.

Darren pays for his shep's pie and doughnut, and then I see him looking round for somewhere to sit. I stare down at the custard stains on the table-top at first so as not to seem too eager, but then force myself to look up and smile at him. He sees me and starts to walk across. My insides start turning over and I hang on to the edge of the table for support. I can feel myself starting to go red.

'Hello,' he says and smiles. He's even got lovely teeth. 'What's the shep's pie like?'

'Foul.'

'That makes a change.' He takes all the things off his tray and sits down opposite. He slides the tray on to the empty chair between us, sorts his cutlery out and pours himself a beaker of water. I hate plastic beakers. They have them in nursery schools.

'Have you seen the list?' he says, smiling. He has a fantastic smile.

'What list?' I'm eating my doughnut now at about three crumbs a minute. It must be the world record for the slowest time anybody's ever taken to eat a synthetic school doughnut. I think they make them out of fibreglass.

'About the play.' He dives into the shep's pie with his knife and fork as though he's afraid of it leaping up and savaging him. He's probably right.

I pour myself a plastic beakerful of water and try to keep calm. 'What about it?'

'A list of people that are in the play. It's up on the notice board – been there since break, I think.'

I start to ask him and then stop myself. It seems unlucky somehow. There's no need anyway. He looks up at me and smiles. 'You're in it,' he says.

An instant of happiness. It's not often I feel like this. 'Are you in it?' I ask him.

He nods. His mouth is full of shepherd's pie.

'What part have you got, then?'

Darren grunts a bit and then takes a drink of water. 'It doesn't mention any parts,' he says. He looks round as if he wants to make sure there's nobody looking and then carries on a bit quieter, 'I don't think it's going to be that sort of play.'

I don't know what he's on about. 'How do you mean?' I ask him.

'When Miss Hoggit organized those auditions I reckon she thought we were going to be reading Shakespeare and learning lines – you know, that sort of stuff. I heard

Miss Gloucester talking about it to the chap who does the lighting. She's going to do it how she wants.'

'Won't we be havin' proper parts, then?'

'I don't know. The first rehearsal's at half-twelve, though. We'll find out then, I suppose.'

Oh no. 'Today?'

'Yes. Why?'

I swear out loud. So loudly in fact that one of the dinner ladies looks up, glares at me and nearly drops her chip basket in the custard. I could strangle Gertie Runt. I could really. I hate her. I suck my cheeks in the way I do when I'm livid and stare down at the table.

'What's up?'

'I'm in detention this dinner-time,' I tell him. 'Half-past twelve. Gertie Runt's keeping me in.'

'Oh, that's stupid. You're not going, are you?'

'No.'

I spend the next seven and a half minutes searching round the school for Gertie Runt to tell her that I won't be coming to her stupid detention. Of course she's nowhere about. She must be hiding from me. And I've gone and left Darren in the dining-room when I could be sitting next to him and talking. On our own. That's just typical.

It's just gone half-past twelve and I don't want to be late for the very first practice so I grab my jeans and T-shirt out of my locker and belt off down to the basement. That's another decent thing about Drama. They let you do it in civilized clothes.

When I get down there, they've started already. It's Relaxation. I say sorry to Miss Gloucester for being late, and creep across to a space and sit down. Everybody else has got their heads down and their eyes shut. I join in.

'. . . the air around you is thick and murky and you have to grope your way through it . . . tentatively . . . step by step. Remember that you cannot see . . . in this new and strange environment you are completely blind . . . I want you to stand up now and slowly begin to make your way through the thick, dense atmosphere . . .'

I gradually clamber to my feet and begin to find myself. Find the fog around me, thick and clinging. Find it difficult to move. Slowly and tentatively, I put my arm out, feeling through the fog . . .

'. . . and when you encounter another moving person, reach out and touch them . . . reassure them that you're there . . . and then, without opening your eyes, stand facing each other . . .'

I move forward . . . clumsily . . . shuffling along with my eyes closed. Feeling my way with my arms stretched out . . . pushing aside the denseness. Something brushes past me. I stop. We grasp each other eagerly. Welcoming. I don't know who it is. We stand and face each other . . .

'And now, very slowly and gently, I want you to reach up and touch each other. Make sure you keep your eyes closed. Remember that the other person is blind . . . they cannot see you . . . they may be feeling nervous or frightened . . . try to be gentle with them. Reassuring . . .'

Hands reach up to my shoulders. Firm hands, large and strong. They rest awhile on my shoulders and then the fingers move . . . gently, stroking the bottom of my neck. I stand transfixed. I don't want to move. I just want to stand there. Wallowing. Passive. Absorbing sensations. The fingers move upwards to my face . . . searching for my mouth . . . touching my ears. I force myself to raise my hand and touch their face . . . the chin feels harsh and rough . . .

'Imagine that when you get home you will be asked to paint a picture of this person and this is your only way of knowing what their features are like. Relax and let your hands explore their face . . . remember that they might be feeling nervous . . .'

I raise my fingers to the cheeks and find them strangely

smooth and soft. The nose is high . . the hair streaks down across the forehead . . . I wonder what colour hair he has . . .

'. . . remember that they trust you . . .'

Fingers moving up to my eyelids. Gently. Smoothly. Stroking my closed eyelids. Tracing the line of my eyebrows. Brushing the hair from my forehead. Finger-tips touching my eyelashes. Trusting. Sensual. Let it go on. Let it go on for ever . . .

'I think you've gone far enough there . . .' You can tell Miss Gloucester's smiling. 'Move away and find yourself another partner.'

It's got to be Darren. This time it's got to be. I open my eyes ever so slightly to make sure I'm walking towards him and I'm surprised to find I'm near the door. I can't see him.

'It must be tempting to open your eyes,' Miss Gloucester says, 'but I insist you keep them closed . . .'

She must have seen me.

'If you can't keep your eyes closed, then you'll have to sit out.'

I'll keep them closed. I hear the sound of the door opening and it's tempting to look, but I don't. You need discipline in Drama. She's always telling us that.

I grope around me and straightaway find myself touching someone else. They seem tense and rigid. Hands by their sides. Last time I was nervous. Now I feel more confident. I reach out and touch the arm gently, just below the elbow I think. Still there's no response. I move around and stand facing her. I think it's a her. She's wearing a jumper, a soft woollen one. That's odd.

'Remember that this person might be feeling nervous.'

I have to be gentle. I stand there, poised, and reach my arms up. I rest my hands upon her shoulders. She's very tall. I wait a few seconds to give her time to gain confidence, but still there's no movement from her. I'm going to move my fingers up and over her face. Gently. Delicately. I start to touch her with my fingertips, just lightly brushing the skin of her neck and chin. Then I half collapse with shock. The skin is flabby; wrinkled; old. It's hanging in folds round her neck.

I let my hands drop. Horrified. I can't believe it. I look downwards at the floor, and then I open my eyes and nearly faint with shock. I realize now what happened when I heard the door open. Standing in front of me I see a pair of yellow platform-soled shoes. Vomit-yellow. Made of worm-skin. I force myself to look upwards at the face that's scowling down at me in horror. Gertie Runt.

4

'Come not between the Dragon and his wrath.'

(Lear, Act I, Scene 1)

Her eyes are blazing down at me and she keeps opening and closing her mouth as if the words are stuck inside it. She's speechless. Her face is slowly turning purple and she looks as though she's going to murder me. It ought to be hilarious but I'm petrified. I know I'll laugh about it afterwards, but not today. Not just yet anyway. She opens her mouth again and looks as if she's ready to explode. I'm nearly paralytic.

Then, a fantastic thing happens. Miss Gloucester, who's been watching all this, comes over and actually takes Gertie Runt by the arm to lead her out. Gertie looks horrified. Her eyes are blazing now at Miss Gloucester. She puts her hand on Miss Gloucester's arm as if she's about to try a half-Nelson or swing her round into a Boston Crab. All the rest of the class still have their eyes shut and they're missing all this. It's great. Miss Gloucester leads Gertie by the arm and takes her to the door. Pushes her really. Gertie's furious.

Miss Gloucester gets her outside and shuts the door before she says anything. At first it's so quiet that you can't hear what they're talking about, but then their voices get louder and louder and you can hear all of it. Most of the kids open their eyes and look at each other; they're a bit embarrassed when they see who they've been touching up. I sit down with my back to the door and pretend I'm not listening. But really my ears are standing out on stalks.

'You can hardly call this *practising a play*,' Gertie's voice is wailing. 'They were all groping around like drunken snowmen. I saw them. That's not acting. It's . . . it's . . .'

'It's building up trust and confidence ready for Improvisation.' Miss Gloucester's voice is firm and strong as if she knows what she's talking about. 'And, to get back to your earlier point, that notice has been up since break. Rebecca knew she had to come here when you told her about the detention.'

'Then she should have asked me for permission. Discipline has to come first, Miss Gloucester,' Gertie snarls like a strangled serpent. 'She must have realized that a detention would have precedence. We must get our priorities right.'

The kids in the room all start making a noise now, laughing and calling out comments like, 'Scrap!' and, 'Put the boot in!' Timothy Trotter stands up and does a stupid impression of Gertie Runt squealing, 'We must get our priorities right,' in a posh, squeaky voice. I can hardly hear what they're saying any more. I wish they'd all shut up. I can just hear Gertie say, 'Well, you certainly won't have heard the last of this incident, Miss Gloucester,' as though Miss Gloucester's a second-year moron caught smoking in the lav. I'm glad I'm not a teacher.

Then the door opens behind me and Gertie pushes her snout through. 'Rebecca O'Leary!' she says, spitting my name at me as though it's a slug she's nearly swallowed on her lettuce.

I turn around and stare at her. I don't even bother to stand up.

'Report to Miss Hoggit's office at four o'clock,' she grunts. 'I think she'll know how to deal with you.'

'Stupid cow,' I mutter, as she shuts the door behind her. She doesn't hear, or she pretends not to. We carry on.

English is the last lesson on Tuesdays and it's my job to

take all the poetry books back to the stockroom at four o'clock. Actually, I did *offer* to take the books back, but how was I to know Streaky Bacon'd take me up on it? The only job I normally do at four o'clock is go home. So then I have to collect all my homework books out of my locker and, by the time I've been to the toilet and got washed and given my hair a brush and set off down to Miss Hoggit's office, I see it's just gone quarter-past four. The offices are all locked up. It's not my fault. She must have gone home.

Tuesday is the day I take the papers round, so I call to buy some sausages on the way home from this shop called Horace Oglet's, where we have an account. That means that I don't have to pay for any of the shopping but they write down in a book how much we owe and then, when he remembers, he calls in and pays the bill. I'm talking about my father, by the way. I say *when he remembers* because sometimes Horace sighs and looks at me as if I'm something that's just crawled out from underneath his toe-nail when I reach the check-out and say, 'It's me, Mr Oglet,' instead of reaching for my purse the way his other customers do.

I hate having to go in Oglet's shop because of something that happened the other week. I don't think I shall ever forget it. What happened was that Horace told me, in front of a whole shopful of customers, that we hadn't paid the bill for five weeks. I nearly died. I think he'll let it go for a month, but five weeks he decides is a bit too much. It wasn't my fault. I felt my cheeks go burning red and everybody in the shop turned round and stared at me. Then there was a terrible silence with everybody glaring, and even the tins of peas and baked beans piled near the sides of the check-out seemed to be formed out of hundreds of tiny green and orange eyes. All staring. I was nearly crying when I got outside.

At home afterwards I asked him if we could start an

account at a different shop because I didn't want to set foot in Horace Oglet's ever again, but he said we couldn't. He said you had to be good customers to open an account. If we were good customers though, I thought, I'd hate to think what Horace Oglet's bad ones were like.

Anyway, I get the sausages and Horace smiles at me and mutters something about the weather looking up, so I think perhaps we must have just paid him. I wish I could forgive him for causing me so much embarrassment the other week, but I can't. I squash the sausages into the bottom of my schoolbag and trundle back home.

As I was saying, I take this paper round on Tuesdays. It's called *The Advertiser* and it's free. I get two pounds fifty, and, if the weather's really terrible, I get thirty pence extra. Usually the weather's all right. You might think two pounds fifty sounds a lot of money, but then you ought to try going round all the houses on our estate. There are too many papers to take all of them on Tuesdays, so I just finish off on a Wednesday. It's a lot of work but I need the cash because I'm saving up to have my hair permed.

Now I realize that this fashion might not last for very long, but at the moment everybody that I know is having a frizzy perm. I wasn't keen on them at first – I thought it looked as though people had had an electric shock with their hair frizzled out like sizzled seaweed. But you know how fashions grow on you. And when you haven't changed your hair style since the second ice age started melting, you begin to wonder if you might be getting a little bit behind the times. In fact, if I get any more old-fashioned, I'll be waking up one morning and finding myself inside a glass case in a museum. Fossilized.

A perm costs ten pounds fifty and I've got eight pounds seventy-five saved up. I have to buy all my own things so it's not easy to save. I hardly ever buy records or magazines or anything like that, and it's a good job I'm not all that interested in buying lots of expensive clothes or make-up. I could never afford any.

When I come back from delivering the papers, I take my money upstairs and put it in my money-box before I go to bed. I might look a bit big to have a money-box but this one is very special. My mum gave it to me and it's the one she used to have when she was a little girl. It's like a Swiss chalet made out of wood with a slot in the top for the money. There are figures standing in the garden: a man and a woman and a little cat, all carved out of wood and painted. And if you wind it up it plays a tune. I hardly ever wind it up because you get fed up of listening to the same tune but, like I say, it's a very special money-box – not like having an old fat plastic pig or something. I count the money and it comes to eleven pounds twenty-five and then I go to bed. He's still out at the pub but I don't care. I think about how I'll look with my hair permed and about the disco at the youth club on Saturday. I've hardly ever been before but Darren goes. I hope my hair will look all right. I used to say my prayers but I don't now. I switch out the light and go to sleep.

5

'The weight of this sad time we must obey;
Speak what we feel, not what we ought to say.'
(Edgar, Act V, Scene III)

It's afternoon break before Miss Hoggit sends for me.

On the door of her office, there are three notices that light up. One says ENTER, the next says PLEASE WAIT, and the last one says COME BACK LATER. I don't know why she can't just shout like anybody else. It would be a good idea for teachers who can't talk, but how many deputy heads are there with no voice? Not many. Her voice is like a wailing warthog. I can't think of anybody who needs talking lights less than she does.

I knock on the door. There's no reply. I shudder and knock again. Nothing's lit up yet. She doesn't have a light that says GET LOST or DROP DEAD. That's what would light up on my door.

What if *she's* dropped dead? I imagine her, collapsed on the carpet in the middle of the room, her fingers outstretched towards the talking light switch, not quite able to reach it . . . her throat rattling . . . her eyes glaring at the ceiling . . . her greasy red lips gasping open, waiting for the kiss of life. Ugh!

A finger taps me sharply on the shoulder. I jump. It feels like a warthog's toe-nail. 'Come inside, Rebecca.' She bustles smartly past me into her room. She's just been to the bog. I take a deep breath and go in.

I think about those schoolboy stories . . . *Billy Bunter,* is it? . . . where they get six of the best. We don't get six of the best at our school. We get talks. They're foul. I sit down opposite her desk and stare at her and watch her false teeth starting to rattle. I don't know why she couldn't get a larger size – or make her mouth shrink. Perhaps she had her false teeth made several years ago and her mouth's grown wider since with exercise. She's always nattering on about something. I try not to listen whilst she warthogs on about my work and how I never do any, and something called my attitude to school, and something else she calls insolence. I don't know what she's talking about. Like I say, I try not to listen. I wish her false teeth would fall out.

Suddenly, there's a silence and I realize that she's asked me a question. I've got no idea what she was talking about, so of course I don't know what to say. I rest my hand on my chin to try and look as though I'm thinking, but it's not easy. Perhaps she'll ask me again.

'Well?' Her eyes stare hard at me as though they're radioactive and can read inside my skull.

'I . . . er . . . I don't know.'

She starts nagging again and this time I really try to listen, but I just don't want to hear any of it. It's all about me and how foul I am. I think I'd rather have the rack. I struggle to remember what it was that I was thinking about before – what it was that took my mind off everything, but she's staring at me again. Her eyes are boring into my skull like laser beams and I have to look away. I wish I'd brought my hankie now. I try to think about having my hair permed on Saturday and going to the youth club disco. I try to think what clothes I'll wear . . . anything to get my mind off *her* . . . but all the time I know her eyes are glaring at me . . . trying to break me down. This must be what the Gestapo were like in the War. Oh God, I hope I don't start crying. I don't want to show myself up.

'What do you want to do when you leave school?' she

asks me. She even makes *that* sound threatening.

But I know about that one. I'm supposed to say a posh job like Prime Minister or a crematorium assistant, then she'll tell me all the qualifications you need and how hard you've got to work for them. I don't want any qualifications. Just leaving school, that's all I want. I don't want any certificates. It'll be like coming out of prison. You don't need a certificate for that; it's exciting enough on its own. I sniff hard. 'I'm not bothered,' I say. 'I don't know.'

'Well, that's just typical, isn't it, Rebecca?'

I'm not supposed to answer that. I just have to look ashamed. It's quite easy. I just wish it was over with, though. I wipe my nose a bit with the end of my cardi and stare at the carpet as though it's just come rocketing in from outer space.

'Typical.' She spits the word out in disgust. Her voice has turned really nasty now. It was pretty foul to start off with. 'I suppose a girl like you would be happy to end up tied to the kitchen sink with two or three children to look after and no career to look forward to. There are women like that you know, Rebecca . . .' She lets my name slide off the end of her tongue like a lump of poisonous slime . . . 'women who stay at home all day long and cook and wash up and cook some more and wash up again and polish their furniture every fortnight . . .'

I clench my fists hard and suck my cheeks in. I know there are women like that. She doesn't need to tell me about it. My mother was one.

' . . . and then in the evening they sit down on their backsides and get out their knitting and . . .'

I clutch the bottom of my cardi in my fist and think about my mother knitting it for me. She used to make all of my jumpers and cardi's. She used to be very good at knitting. When I was little she made clothes for my teddy bear and all my stuffed animals – little bobble hats and knitted scarves and waistcoats. One day she even knitted a stripy trunk warmer for my stuffed elephant with all the bits of different coloured wool she had left over. It was all rainbow-coloured and . . .

'. . . and that's all there is to their lives, Rebecca . . .'

She used to sit in this special chair by the window, looking out over the garden. Especially when she started to be poorly. She used to look up and smile at me and wave when I walked down the path on my way home from school, and I can still see her face inside my mind and remember every detail. It was a beautiful face. Just a little bit wrinkled on her forehead and round the corners of her eyelids when she smiled. She used to smile a lot. I loved my mother very much.

'. . . and that's all there is in their lives, Rebecca: cooking and knitting.' She snarls these words at me as if they're the most obscene expressions in the English language. 'Knitting and cooking and washing-up . . .'

I see the jars of blackberry jam, piled up high and labelled in the pantry. Each with its neat little label edged in blue. I see her face again as she stands by the cooker stirring the jam in a big cauldron. The tears start squeezing their way into the corner of my eyes now and I keep trying to blink them away so that The Hog won't notice that I'm crying, but then I feel them rushing faster, overflowing like a blocked-up gutter.

I rub my eyes with the end of my cardi sleeve as if they are just smarting a bit or something, but then I see the picture of my mother again and this time she's knitting the cardigan for me and measuring the sleeves against me to be sure they'll fit me properly. And the sobs start heaving their way up inside my throat. I swallow hard and try to force them back, but this great mound of sadness is struggling to erupt and it's unbearable. My bottom lip starts trembling and my shoulders begin to shake. The Hog isn't taking any notice of me at all. For all she cares I could just be a screaming earwig she's trodden on in the rain. She keeps on strangling me with words, wrapping them tighter and tighter round my throat. I can feel myself being choked . . .

'. . . and that's just how you'll finish up, Rebecca. You mark my words. You throw away your chances and you'll finish up tied to the kitchen sink, a parasite on society . . . an old woman at thirty . . . a slovenly mess . . .'

That's it. I've had enough. I can't take any more now. Before I even know what's happening, I find myself standing up and facing her. My cheeks are burning red with hatred and my fists are clenched as tight as rocks with strength I never knew I owned. My eyes are wet with salty tears, but I can see her shock-filled face. She's staring at me open-mouthed, leaning backwards in her chair and gaping up at me. She's frightened. I could kill her. I feel so strong with all the hate that's burning up inside me and she can see the hatred glaring in my eyes. She knows I could kill her.

I open my mouth and stare her straight between the eyes. My voice is loaded with resentment. I hate her. 'I hate you!' I shout at her. And then I take a deep breath and scream out in a voice they must be able to hear right out in the playground, 'Just bloody well leave me alone!' My voice is strong and powerful. It frightens me. She looks up, shocked and angry, but says nothing. She's speechless.

I stare at her hard to show I'm not ashamed of what I've said and I narrow my eyes to show I hate her, then turn to leave the room.

'How d . . .' she starts off, but I don't wait to hear the rest. I've had enough. I hold my head up as I walk out into the corridor and slam the door. The sound vibrates around the hallway and I start to stumble along the corridor. The bell's just going for the end of break and kids are storming into school. I feel as if I'm going to explode with the blood still pounding away inside my head. I can't stand it any more. I shall just have to go home.

6

'Who alone suffers, suffers most i' the mind,
Leaving free things and happy shows behind.'

(Edgar, Act III, Scene VI)

I try to keep the tears back as I stumble down the street, telling myself that I can cry when I get home if I want to. I wish I'd made the bed now. I feel numb but shaking still, as if I've just been run over by an electric road drill. I stagger in through the front door and put my hand on the bannister to steady myself as I walk upstairs, and then I collapse on top of the heap of covers on my bed. Strangely enough, I don't feel as though I want to cry any longer. I just feel drained. Washed out. I don't want to do anything. I lie there on the crumpled sheets with my head underneath the big dollop of blankets and I know that I could make myself cry if I started to think about my mother again, but I don't. I just lie completely still and think about nothing.

And, although my head is empty of thoughts, my mind is saturated with emotion. The anger and the hatred have flooded out now, and washing in behind them comes this sea of loneliness. A loneliness so deep and vast you couldn't measure it. It seems to stretch for ever. It terrifies me.

I try to flush it away, the loneliness, by concentrating on the nothingness in my head. It's not easy. When I was little, my mother told me once about how you can think about nothing. I used to go to Quaker Meetings when I was small because Mum was Quaker. All the children used to come into the Meeting for ten minutes just before the end and would sit there with their parents in the

Silence. I used to fidget about. It seemed ages to me, sitting for ten minutes without saying anything or moving, and Mum used to look at me and smile and pat my hand. I was only very small, you see.

One day she explained to me about the Silence. She said it was like when you played Pass the Parcel at a party and took the different layers off the parcel. One layer was the noises in the room and you had to shut your mind to them. Another layer was the people; you got distracted if you kept looking at them all. It was easiest to sit with your eyes closed. The next layers were all your thoughts, and these went on and on because once you'd got rid of one lot of thoughts, others kept coming. You had to empty your mind of all your thoughts and, if you did that, you could talk to God.

I don't think that God ever had a chance to talk to me because my mind was never empty for more than a few seconds at once. But now, lying here, I suddenly know what it's like to think of nothing: a deep emptiness. It's a shame I don't want to talk to God because it would be a perfect chance for Him to get a word in edgeways. I drift off to sleep instead.

When I wake up, I feel much better. The room is peaceful and my mind seems sharp and clearer now. I lie in bed for a while, just thinking.

After a few minutes, I get up and walk over to the shelf. I take down the pieces of paper, pages torn out of my school exercise books, where I've been scribbling down these notes – writing about what's happened to me. I read them through and decide what I'm going to do with them: I'm going to make them into a book. I take down my notepad and I spend ten minutes thinking of a title, but I can't decide, so then I make up my mind to leave it until the end. I'll be able to see what it's been about best when it's finished.

Then I begin to copy the notes out, all of them in my best writing, checking the spellings in my dictionary. Yes, I decide, I'm going to write a book – a book about me and everything that's happened to me. I think I'll have to alter the names of some of the people, though, particularly the ones at school, otherwise I might get into trouble for writing about them.

Some of the notes I'll copy out just as they're written; others I'll add bits on to. I'm going to write something every day, I tell myself. It'll be better than just a diary or an English essay. It'll be my life story for as long as I want to write about myself – as long as I want people to know . . .

After I've finished all this hard work, I decide to go for a walk to the shops and treat myself to a magazine and some sweets. I think about making my bed before I go out, but decide against it because your brain can't cope with too much activity at once. Then I walk across and open my money-box, have a count-up of the cash and take out twenty-eight pence.

On my way down to the shops, I start thinking about going back to school tomorrow and I start to panic. My insides sag like Mickey Mouse when he's swallowed a cannon-ball whenever I think about school. I can just imagine them calling me out of Assembly, a high voice screeching down the microphone like an electronic hyena: 'Miss Hoggit would like to see Rebecca O'Leary in her office straight after Assembly . . .' All the kids would turn round and stare at me and I'd stand there, bright red, padlocked to the spot like a paraplegic beetroot. I don't know what I'm going to do.

I remember when I was in the second year and we had these readings in Assembly from a book called *Great Heroes*, and they were all about famous soldiers who'd killed a lot of people in the War. I didn't think it was right because I don't really believe in killing people, and when I told my mum about it, she came up to school the very next morning, first thing, to see the headmaster. I was a bit surprised because she didn't usually like to make a fuss, at school. I don't know what she said to him, but we didn't have any more readings at all from *Great Heroes* after that. We had 'The Good Samaritan' again for the nine hundred and thirty-first time, and that story about the poodle that jumps out of the train window.

But I wish Mum could come up to school now. I wish she could tell them for me . . . tell them to stop picking on me and saying foul things about me all the time. Some kids have even got a father who'd do that. Take a morning off work and walk into the headteacher's office in their best suit. All smiles and charm. He wouldn't do that. He'd have a hangover and be chain-smoking. He'd show me up. He'd never take a morning off work to help me.

I come out of the newsagent's with my magazine and chocolate and I think again a bit harder. It might be possible. It sounds a bit stupid, but really I'm getting desperate. There's going to be a fantastic row at school tomorrow and, if I could just persuade him to come up, it might get me out of it. Or perhaps he could phone them? Just tell them how upset I've been and ask them to stop getting at me. If he'd only have a quick word on the telephone, it wouldn't give them much chance to moan at him about all the things I've been doing wrong at school for the last nine million years. He might just do it. It's asking him that's the problem. I don't think I've asked him for anything since I used to scream to have my nappies changed.

Whilst I'm working out what I might say to him, I open the door of Oglet's shop and pick up my wire basket. It occurs to me that I could make him something special for tea to put him in a good mood, and so I have a look at the cake mixes. Most of them have a list of instructions as long as an alligator's backside. It'd be quicker to go to the library for a recipe book. Then I see one that looks easier. PETUNIA ORKY'S CAKE MIX it says on the top of the packet.

ROCK BUNS
Just add butter, one egg, milk and sultanas
for a delicious, mouthwatering recipe.

I nearly crack out laughing. I'm sure you don't put anything else into rock buns except flour. They must be charging you thirty-two and a half pence for a few mingy tablespoonsful of self-raising flour. I decide they've got such a nerve that I pick up the packet and plonk it into my wire basket with a box of sultanas from the next shelf.

I hope he's going to appreciate this. I buy a bag of potatoes as well and a packet of frozen pork chops. Then a tin of apple sauce to go with them. My mother would've had a fit. She'd never have bought fruit in a tin. Especially not apples. I smile at Horace Oglet on my way out and he nearly has a heart attack. I think the last time he saw me smiling was the day I cut my first tooth – about fourteen years ago.

7

'Some villain hath done me wrong.'

(Edgar, Act I, Scene II)

Well, it's a quarter to seven and he hasn't come home yet. I hate him.

I pick up the plate with his pork chops on and the mashed potatoes nestling in the apple sauce and I bung it on a shelf in the oven. I kick the door shut. Hard. Then I sit back down at the table and decide that I might as well treat myself to a rock bun with my cup of tea. Ugh! I nearly choke myself. They taste foul. As hard as concrete with bits of burnt sultanas poking out and not even a soft mudgy part in the middle. They're just like rocks.

I've been sitting here like an ice-cream salesman in a mortuary, wading through my tea by myself and working out what I'm supposed to say to him when he comes home. Going over it in my mind:

'I hope I haven't burnt your apple sauce, Dad. I'd like to ask you a favour . . .

'There's something I'd like to talk to you about, Dad . . . dunk your rock bun in your tea if it needs softening up a bit . . .

'I came home from school a bit early today. I swore at Miss Hoggit and I . . .'

I slide the remnants of the rock bun into the rubbish bin and plonk my plate down into the sink. I can't be bothered washing up. It's time for me to take the rest of the papers out now.

I sweep the crumbs off the tablecloth and put his knife

and fork straight. His mug's already waiting with the tea bag in the bottom. If I'm lucky, he'll perhaps still be in a good mood when I get back—if his tea's not been burnt up to a frazzle. As I put my coat on ready to go out, I'm conscious again of that sunken cannon-ball feeling inside me. And it's more than just the rock bun. It's like an awareness of disaster. As if I know I've got to face something dreadful and doom-laden and I don't even want to think about it. Like sitting in your examination desk or in the dentist's waiting-room, every foul pig in the world waiting round the corner to leap out at you and trample you to a pancake. Walking into my mother's ward at the hospital and knowing she was going to die. But I can't think about it. I'm not made out of rock buns, you see. Just a masticated mess of pain and misery. Nerves as tough as splintered glass; muscles hard as jelly. I slam the door behind me as I walk out into the rain.

I come back home from delivering the papers and wonder what kind of mood he's in. I've been going through this conversation so many times in my mind now that the words are nearly worn out already. I imagine them hanging in the air above me like a monorail track – words with deep ruts engraved down the middle where I've motored backwards and forwards across them:

'Was your dinner all right, Dad? I'm sorry that the rock buns were a bit crozzled . . .

'I wonder if you could help me with something? I've got this little problem at school, Dad . . .'

Of course I might get home and find the house is empty, but he doesn't usually go out on Wednesdays. He's usually broke. Friday's his pay-day so he's normally spent up after the week-end. He's hopeless with money. I could manage it better by myself.

I take a deep breath and try to turn the handle on the

back door but it's locked. I fish in my purse for the key. I unlock the door and walk inside the kitchen and there's still the tea things scattered on the table and a pile of dirty dishes in the sink. I walk straight through and into the living-room and it's empty. I take off my coat and hang it up.

He's gone out. He's eaten his tea and left all the washing-up for me to do. Here I am waiting to talk to him for the first time in ninety million years and he's picked himself up and gone out. I hate him.

I thump myself upstairs to my bedroom and that enormous weight is still heaving around inside my stomach like a pregnant elephant. I open the door and walk inside my room and straightaway I feel upset. I can see he's been inside here. The bed's been straightened. It's just like having burglars. I hate him coming into my room. It's my room. All mine. And there's nothing else in this house that belongs to me and he's got no right to come here. It's my bed. He's got no right to make it. If I want my bed all straight and looking as if it's in a hospital with the sheets turned back, I'll do it like that. But I don't. It looks like a coffin. I'm old enough to keep my own bed straight you see, when I want to, but sometimes I just don't feel like it and I can't stand somebody else messing my things about. Why didn't he wash up instead, if he wanted to make himself useful?

I sit down on the bed and scowl at the Snoopy poster on the wall. Then I reach into my back pocket and take out the change that's still there from when I went to buy the chocolate and walk across to post it in my money-box. The money-box has moved.

It hasn't moved far. Just a few centimetres so it's balanced right on the edge of the shelf, but far enough for me to know that someone's touched it. I always keep it right at the back of the shelf, flat against the wall, and there's even a little oblong printed in the dust so you can tell straightaway that it isn't in its proper place. I hate anybody touching my things.

I have a horrible feeling as well that I know what's happened – why my money-box has moved. Twice before I've opened it and found some money missing and both times on a Tuesday. He's stolen a pound note out of my money-box for going drinking with and then, before I've had the courage to ask him about it, he's gone and put it back. That's the sort of father he is. I suck my cheeks in hard, take a deep breath and start to undo the tiny metal fastener at the back that makes the little chalet's roof lift off.

The money's gone. Well, most of it. I take out the pound notes that are left and start counting them out on my knee. There's five pounds ninety-seven pence left. He's stolen five pounds from me! I can hardly believe it. I've heard about some kids stealing money from their parents – taking change out of their mother's purse and that sort of thing – and I think that's disgusting. But have you ever heard of a man stealing money from his own daughter? It's revolting. I don't know how he can do it.

I sit there on the edge of the bed for a few moments, counting the pound notes over again in case perhaps I've missed a few. Turning the little wooden chalet over in my hands in case the money has got lost inside it somewhere, and then I sit there stroking the little painted cat, sandwiched in the painted garden between the painted man and woman and I feel as though I've just been knocked down by a bulldozer.

It's a weird kind of feeling. I don't feel angry and furious, as if I want to throw things round the room, and I don't want to bang my head on the wall and start screaming, and I don't even want to cry. I just feel hollow somehow. As if I don't have any feelings. Like the wooden, painted figures in front of the little Swiss chalet.

Emotions just wash through me like the sea inside an empty shell. I feel numb.

I close down the lid of the wooden chalet and I slide the little fastener into place at the back. Then I wind up the key underneath, just a few turns, and whilst the tune is playing I post the money that's left, piece by piece, in through the opening at the top. Each pound note and coin dropping in carefully like I remember posting my party invitations once when I could hardly reach the slot in the post-box, waiting for each one to fall before I posted the next one through. It's a long time now since I had a birthday party.

I listen to the tune winding down for a few seconds. There's something safe and comfortable about the clock-work music. It reminds me of being little again – of having animals on my wall-paper and a doll's house and a teddy bear under my pillow. You always know what's happening with a musical box. You can hear every note inside your head before it plays and know that it's never going to come out any different. The same sounds every time, just as you imagine them. Just as you expect they're going to be. You can trust a musical box.

When the very last note's finished playing, I walk downstairs. I don't want to see my father now. I want to finish all the clearing away and washing-up so I can be out of the way upstairs when he comes back home. I clear the things away quickly from the table and put the dishes in the sink. I put the kettle on for some hot water and give the tablecloth a shake outside. There's a soggy tea bag on the draining board which I pick up with the very tip of my finger and thumb like a – well, you know as well as I do what soggy tea bags are like – and take it over to the pedal bin.

When I press the lid up on the bin, I see the tea that I've cooked for him, lying there scraped on top of the potato peelings and the empty cat food tin and the remnants of my rock bun. I feel a sense of shock for a few seconds, as if I've just seen a dead rat or something, but then I slop the soggy tea bag on top and close the lid down. What else could I have expected?

When the washing-up's finished and the table cleared, I take myself upstairs to bed. I'm feeling very tired so I think I'll drop straight off to sleep, but of course I don't. Just when I'm nearly asleep at last, I hear this scuffling noise under the bed and then the cat creeps out and clambers on top of the eiderdown. Our cat's always disappearing. I keep expecting him to have got run over or lost. Or snatched up by one of those vans that are supposed to tour the streets looking for stray animals for vivisection. But I think they'd take one look at our Scruffbag and run. Our cat's about as attractive as Dracula's mother-in-law after an all-night party.

I drag myself out of bed, take the cat downstairs and put it out and then, when I've climbed back into bed, I find that I don't really want to go to sleep. I start to think instead.

Like I said, I don't want to cry any more or start screaming – I just still feel this numbness inside me as if I've turned to stone or something, and going through my head are things my mother used to tell me.

When I asked my mother about God, she told me that it wasn't someone in the sky who made the world and animals and everything. But she said that God was something that moved inside people – an invisible force – and she said there was something of God in everyone. She said that if we only searched deeply enough and hard enough, we could find the God that lived inside us and we could find the God inside each other.

But that's where she was wrong. Because if she thought that there was any God inside *him*, she was making the world's biggest mistake since the invention of the atom bomb. There's no more God in him than there's sunshine in a coffin. I hate him.

It's quite a long time later when I hear him coming home and I wish I wasn't listening because really I intended to be fast asleep. I don't want to know. I try to bury my head in the pillow with my hands across my ears and shut my mind to everything that's happening. Like I said, I don't want to know. I don't want to hear him staggering down the road like a lost child, moaning under his breath and leaning on the neighbour's fence whilst he tries to remember where he is. It's a part of my life I'd rather get away from.

But I can't. I take my hands away from my ears and I find myself listening. It's like watching a horror film that you know will give you nightmares but you can't stop watching and it's part of my life. It's fascinating. I hear his footsteps scraping on the pavement like a cripple and I hear him muttering inanities and groaning as he breathes heavily and sighs like an animal in pain. I hear him pausing by the kerbside trying to get his balance and then stumbling forward, and all the time these weird sounds coming from him like a madman. Sounds that normal people never make: groans and cries and whimpering. Then I hear his footsteps just outside the house, dragging along and shuffling. And they stop, pause in front of the wall by the garden and I can imagine him leaning on the wall and bending over towards the flower-bed where the bulbs are just starting to peep through ready for the spring.

And then I hear it. I hold my breath and my heart stops beating for a second. I shiver with horror. He's vomiting. I can hardly bear to listen to it but I force myself. I think of all the neighbours behind their curtains and their neat, pull-down blinds, listening to him retching in the street. Not a quiet, subtle noise as if he's ashamed of what he's doing, but a great intake of breath and a horrendous gargling like an enormous pig being strangled. I squirm in my bed as I cling on to my pillow and I imagine it lying there amongst the crocuses in the garden that my mother used to care for, and him bent double over the wall, staring down, with his face nearly dangling in it.

That's the kind of father I've got.

8

'We are not ourselves
When Nature, being oppress'd, commands the mind
To suffer with the body.'

(Lear, Act II, Scene IV)

The next morning I try not to look at the nauseating splatter in the flower-bed as I set off down the street to go to school. If I look the other way, I tell myself, perhaps the neighbours'll think it's nothing to do with me. Or they might think I'm not bothered about it, as if it's something we've just decided to spread across the crocuses to make the flowers brighter when they come up. Or add a touch of colour to the soil till they do.

'Crocuses not in bloom yet?
Is your front garden looking bleak and empty?
Add a touch of colour to your flower-bed;
Replace valuable nutrients lost from the earth . . .
(Fanfare of trumpets) Der . . . der . . . der . . . dum . . .
da . . .
Add new, colourful vomit.
Vomit? Yes. Choose from exciting rainbow shades of
Orange, yellow and cream . . .
Just phone and ask for Mr Rex O'Leary's special offer
For personal deliveries nightly, fresh from the . . .'

I've left him still in bed. Lying there with his face puffed out and his mouth gaping open like a huge grounded whale. A sick whale. All fat and blubbery.

He used to worry about not being able to stagger in to work in the morning after he'd come home in a stupor, and he'd get me to phone them up and say he had a migraine. Or a bad back. Or gastro something or other that I never used to be able to pronounce properly and is really just a fancy way of saying that you've got the trots. I can say diarrhoea but it's not a word I like to use much down the telephone. Anyway, I think he's past caring now about whether he gets in to work or not. They won't let him keep this job much longer. He must know that as well as I do.

So, I set off to school, and I think several times before I reach the gate of walking straight past and taking myself off somewhere nice for the day. But I decide against it. There's nowhere nice to go.

And of course I'm still worrying about all the things I was worried about yesterday. Just because everything at home's been extra foul, it doesn't mean there's any chance of things being any less foul at school. But one thing about getting to school in the morning is that you can never allow yourself to feel upset because, when they build schools, they make rooms for learning and studying in, and for cooking and eating and storing books and paint in, but there's one thing that everybody wants to do some time at school that they never ever think to build a room for. They never build a room for you to cry in.

I stagger into Assembly and it's as boring as usual. But, you know, before Assembly starts, whilst everybody's waiting all peaceful and quiet in the hall, they always play some music. And sometimes, just sometimes, they play this beautiful music, all haunting and sad, that makes you feel as if you want to cry.

So then it's best if you don't allow yourself to listen. Today, for instance, Sarah Swille's just folding up this crumpled old magazine and squashing it into her pocket, so I ask her if I can borrow it and have a read. Then I won't have to listen to the music. The magazine's all battered and creased because about seventy-nine other people have read it before me.

First of all, I look at Hilary Hock's problem page. All the problems are stupid. They never write up about anything sensible.

> Dear Hilary,
> My little brother is always teasing me.
> What shall I do?

I take my felt-tip pen and write underneath the letter:

Strangle him!

I won't tell you what Hilary Hock's written. It's too ridiculous to contemplate.

The next letter's just as stupid:

> Dear Hilary,
> I get very embarrassed because I
> think my nose is too big . . .

I pick up my felt-tip and scrawl down the side:

Have a head transplant!

I glance across at Sarah to see if she's watching me, but she's looking downwards into her pocket mirror, brushing blue mascara on to her eyelashes. It looks revolting.

> Dear Hilary,
> My problem is that I have a crush
> on my games teacher. I think she's
> really wonderful. Every time
> she . . .

I take my felt-tip out again and write across Hilary Hock's answer:

Go and have your head examined. You must be stupid!

The next letter comes from a girl who's just a great big show-off:

> Dear Hilary,
> My problem is that there are two boys who want to go out with me and I can't decide which one to choose. They are both incredibly handsome. Philip is tall and blond and . . .

Big Head!

I write underneath:

You don't deserve any advice!

The last letter is one that really makes me take notice because it comes from a girl who sounds exactly like me.

> Dear Hilary,
> My problem is that everything in life seems to be going wrong for me. I don't get on at all well with my parents and when I'm at home I feel miserable and depressed all the time. The teachers are always picking on me at school and I find it difficult to get on with my work. I don't have many friends so I often feel lonely and there's nobody I can talk to about my problems. I haven't got a boy friend yet and boys don't seem to find

me very attractive. There is a boy that I like but he doesn't even seem to notice me. Please help me. I'm feeling really desperate and so depressed . . .

Love,
Rosalind

The letter's so sad that it nearly brings tears to my eyes when I read it. The girl who's written it sounds so much like me. I look down quickly to see what sort of advice she's given; any advice to this girl would be useful to me as well.

Dear Ros,
I'm sorry to hear that you're so down in the dumps, but life's not all a bunch of roses, is it? Why not splash out on an exciting new outfit of clothes for the disco on Saturday? (See p. 3 of this mag for some really trendy ideas.) Or what about a way-out new hair-do? (Some of the styles in fashion at the moment are quite exciting – a perm would be just the thing to liven you up!) With a completely different image, you just can't fail to feel on top of the world!

Yours sincerely,
Hilary Hock

I put the magazine down and swear. Quite a few people turn round and glare at me because we're in the middle of the Lord's Prayer by this time. I won't tell you what I said because if I wrote it down they might not let me publish this book when it's finished, but perhaps I'd better tell you that some of my swear words can be pretty revolting.

I notice that some of the teachers are casting dirty glances round the hall, so I put a really shocked expression on my face and turn round as if I'm trying to find who it is that's uttered such foul obscenities in the middle of the prayers. Turning round with a shocked look on your face is the quickest way to get out of trouble. But I suppose you know about that anyway. You should do if you're the sort of person who's going to read this book.

'... for ever and ever, Amen,' crackles the microphone.

'Amen,' I say as loudly as I can without shouting, trying to look religious. I glance back up at the row of teachers again, but now they're all staring into space like a line of gibbons in a moon rocket. There's an empty chair in the middle I notice where Miss Gloucester usually sits. I hope she isn't away because there's a Drama practice again at half-past twelve. I might not see Darren if we have to miss it.

I listen to the microphone whistling on about things that don't concern me, but I listen hard because really I'm expecting it to call out my name to go and see the headmaster or somebody about yesterday. You can never tell whose turn it is to speak down the microphone from our end of the hall. You just hear this voice:

'... and will you please be careful at dinner-time to make sure that no cutlery is placed in the pig swill bin. With the number of knives being found in the pig swill nowadays, people will be buying their bacon ready sliced ...'

A lot of kids laugh at this. I don't. It's about the thirty-seventh time somebody's made that joke since I've been coming to this school.

'... and can we please stop this disgusting habit of bringing chewing-gum into the dining-hall. Several children have been taking chewing-gum out of their mouths and sticking it on the edge of their plates whilst they eat their dinner. Or, worse still, sticking it under the dining-tables. Now, you wouldn't like the job of scraping chewing-gum off the edge of dinner-plates would you? And nor do the dinner ladies ...'

I think I've guessed who the voice belongs to. She'll be moaning on about the school caretaker next ...

'. . . and the school caretaker spent two hours trying to loosen his bristles . . .'

I take out the magazine again and turn over to the next page. There's a quiz called 'How You Rate on a Date' with a picture of a soppy-looking boy and girl arm in arm, grinning at each other. Somebody's already inked in some of their teeth, so I draw a moustache on the girl, square off the boy's head and draw a few stitches on his forehead.

'. . . and what sort of impression do you think it makes on important visitors when they walk out of school with great lumps of it stuck underneath their shoes?'

I take a look at the quiz. About eighteen people have already filled it in; you can read their scores all in different coloured inks in the margin. It'll be most of the retarded girls in our class who've done it; I bet none of them have ever even been on a date.

> 'Your date has booked seats for you at an expensive restaurant, not knowing that you have only just eaten a three course meal. What do you do?'

Sarah Swille's put that she'd eat the meal in the restaurant as well. The fat pig. That's just like her. Amelia Hamlet's put that she'd say she was slimming. That's a prize joke. She's so thin she'd make a stick of spaghetti look overweight. Nobody in their right mind would believe her. I bet none of them have ever been to a posh restaurant anyway – certainly not on a date. They'd be lucky if anybody treated them to a bag of chips and a fish cake from Chippy Later's Chip Shop. Not that anybody's ever taken me out to an expensive restaurant, now I come to think of it.

Whilst I'm looking through the list of answers to see what I can put to these stupid questions, I realize that everybody round about me is standing up and making for the door. Assembly's finished. I fold up the magazine ready to finish the quiz during English, and stand up. I breathe a sigh of relief because nobody's sent for me yet, but I know there's always plenty of time for that later. They like to keep you waiting. I always start looking for Darren when Assembly's over because sometimes I can work it so that I walk out into the aisle just when he's coming over from where the fifth years sit, but today I can't see him. I can tell it's going to be one of those days when nothing turns out right. You know, like every other day.

We're reading this book in English and it's boring. We read it every week. I don't know where he finds such boring books. Whenever I go into a bookshop all the books look really interesting and there's lots of them I'd like to read if I could afford them. He must walk in and say, 'What's the most boring book you've got at the moment? Have you got one that nobody's read for the last sixty-three years?'

And when they find one for him, he buys thirty copies of it and makes us read it every week.

I stand my bag up on the desk in front of me and take out the crumpled magazine.

> 'Whilst watching an exciting horror film at the movies, your date drops the end of his lollipop down the back of the dress of the woman sitting in front of you. Do you:
> a) Pretend you're not with him
> b) Help him to fish it out
> c) Buy him a choc ice instead . . .?'

This quiz gets more ridiculous all the time. I don't know where they get all these stupid questions from.

Still, I study the answers everyone else has put and start trying to decide. Like I say, it keeps you from thinking about things that might affect you.

*

I don't see Darren at dinner-time because our class is late going into the dining-room. Miss Snortelotte kept us behind in the changing-rooms to look for Amelia Hamlet's track suit bottoms which were suspended above her all the time from one of the water pipes up near the ceiling. Sarah had thrown them across whilst Amelia Hamlet was in the showers and they sort of stuck.

'Right, girls!' Miss Snortelotte had bawled, stamping her foot on the wet tiles and splashing dirty water all up the side of my leg. 'You can just stay here until Amelia's bottoms turn up.'

Everybody sat down on the bench and tried not to look at the ceiling. We were all giggling. I made a big show of washing my leg clean again where Snortelotte had splashed it. It's amazing how hard it can be *not* to look at something. Normally you might never look at the ceiling when you're changing after P.E., but just then it was impossible. Out of the corner of my eye, I could see that the track suit bottoms were just beginning to slither down from the pipe immediately over Miss Snortelotte's head.

'I don't know how you expect to find them,' she spluttered, 'sitting there like stuffed dummies. I suppose you expect them to come sailing down from Heaven like a . . .'

She never finished what she was saying because the track suit bottoms suddenly slithered down from the pipes and fell straight on top of her head. You should have seen her face when they landed on her. The empty legs were dangling down in front of her face and she had to push them out of the way before she could scowl at us for laughing. We were hysterical. So that made all the girls in our class late for dinner and they'd only got fish fingers left and I couldn't see Darren anywhere. I hate P.E. teachers.

When I've managed to swallow a tablespoonful of stewed rhubarb and half a cold fish finger, I fetch my jeans and T-shirt out of my locker and walk downstairs to the Drama Workshop. Miss Gloucester smiles at me when I walk in. 'Hello,' I say. 'I thought you weren't here this morning.'

'No, I came late.' And then, when she sees I'm not really satisfied, she adds, 'I went to the hospital.'

I wonder what's the matter with her. She looks all right to me. I'd like to be able to say that I hope it's nothing serious, but I can't. I'm not much good at things like that. I walk away and sit down.

First of all we have Relaxation. Then we sit in a large semicircle together in the middle of the room. The Relaxation works because it makes you feel all peaceful afterwards. I think it's a good idea.

'We're going to start with a scene from the beginning of the play,' Miss Gloucester tells us, sitting cross-legged on the floor facing the circle. 'The King is quite old and he knows he can't live for ever, so he wants to divide his kingdom between his daughters.' She pauses a moment to let this sink in. Being as I'm probably the only person who hasn't read this play, I'm very glad she does. 'In order to show everyone just how much each daughter deserves, he asks them to tell him, in turn, exactly what they think of him.'

A few people smile at this. I find it very puzzling, but Miss Gloucester goes on to choose two of the older girls to be Lear's daughters and Timothy Trotter to be the King.

At first it doesn't go too well. The girls don't seem to understand what to do and Timothy Trotter makes a stupid King. He's small and podgy with a little squeaky voice. I know you've got to use your imagination in Drama but this is ridiculous. In the end, Miss Gloucester has a rummage in the props box and finds a cloak and a miniature cardboard crown that looks as if it was worn by a midget pixie. She sits Timothy Trotter on a big stool with the cloak around his shoulders and the miniature crown balanced on top of his head, and Bernice Berkshire, who's supposed to be his eldest daughter, has to kneel down in front of him and try not to laugh. Timothy frowns hard and glowers at her like a short-sighted Batman. It's hilarious. He's so fat he looks more like a prize piglet than a king. Bernice can hardly keep a straight face.

'Tell me what you think about me,' Timothy Trotter squeaks, waving his arm at Bernice and nearly toppling off the edge of his stool. 'All my kingdoms are to be shared out,' he squeals, waving his other arm over his head to show how far his kingdoms stretch and nearly knocking his cardboard crown flying into the courtiers.

Bernice looks up at his feet dangling in front of her about ten centimetres from the ground and at his lopsided cardboard crown, and tries to put a rapturous expression on her face. She clasps her hands together and looks up at him in admiration. 'I think you're wonderful,' she says. Everybody laughs. I never knew Shakespeare could be so funny.

After a few minutes, Miss Gloucester chooses different people to play the characters and starts to ask us some questions about them. 'Why do you think Lear is doing this?' she asks. 'What's it all for?'

Those kids who've obviously read the play say that really he must have already decided who's going to have which share of the kingdom and this scene is all for show – just to show off how much his daughters think about him. I don't say anything. I suppose they must be right but it all seems very strange to me.

The other people start to get into the scene a lot better. We have a different King Lear called Jonathan who's big and ugly and grins at people as if he'd like to have their heads chopped off. He seems more how you'd expect a king to be. There are two girls whose names I don't know but in the play they're Goneril and Regan, two of Lear's daughters. I don't know how many he has altogether.

Lear stares hard at Goneril and puts on a really tough voice. 'Well?' he asks her.

Goneril flinches a bit. 'It's . . . it's not easy to find words,' she stammers, looking down at the floor, 'to express how much I love you.' A few of the other kids giggle a bit at this, but Goneril carries on without taking any notice of them. 'I worship you,' she says. 'You're like a god; the most wonderful person in the whole world.'

I think she's laying it on a bit thick. It's embarrassing really; it's so false. Nobody could possibly feel like that about their father. I hope that the other daughter, Regan, will try and tone things down a bit, but instead she goes on twice as alarming as her sister:

'Goneril has taken most of the words right out of my mouth,' she says. 'Except that words have just never been thought of to express how deep my love is . . .'

I think it's ridiculous. I don't care how much land your father owns, you shouldn't have to creep like that just to get a share of it. It's worse than your father refusing to leave you any land at all, making you behave like that in public. I wouldn't. I'd rather die. If my father asked me what I thought about him, then I'd tell him. Straight. I'd tell him I hated him. I wouldn't creep like that for anybody.

9

'How sharper than a serpent's tooth it is
To have a thankless child!'

(Lear, Act 1, Scene IV)

I have a sudden burst of energy when I get home so I decide to cook some spaghetti. Usually nowadays we just have some out of a tin, but today I climb up on the stool and reach over right at the back of the top shelf in the cupboard and bring out a dusty old packet of this long spaghetti – the sort that my mother used to make.

You might think that I don't know how to cook spaghetti but I do, because I often used to help Mum. I boil some water in a pan and put some salt in and then, when the water's boiling, I tip half the packet of spaghetti in and very slowly bend it round. You have to wait for the hot water to make the spaghetti soft, you see, before you can curl it round the pan. Then I turn the pan down a bit and start to wash up the breakfast things whilst it's cooking.

I won't tell you exactly what I think about whilst I'm doing the washing-up because I don't want this book to get all sloppy. But Darren came and sat next to me after we'd finished Drama. I allow myself to imagine, just for a few minutes, what I might have said to him if the words had occurred to me at the time, and what he might have said to me, and how things might have developed after that. Nothing really *did* happen of course, but day-dreaming never costs you anything. Except a bit of disappointment.

When I've washed up I look round the kitchen for other things to go in with the spaghetti. Mum used to put onions and mushrooms and grated cheese in with it, but of course we haven't got anything like that, so what I do is open this tin of tomato soup. I pour it in with the spaghetti and stir it round a bit. It'll be better than nothing.

I have a nibble at the spaghetti to work out if it's cooked or not and it doesn't taste too bad – sort of like soggy string – and the next job is to serve it out on two plates. I bring a plate over to the cooker and try to dollop out spoonfuls of spaghetti from the pan but, do you know, it's impossible.

Have you ever tried to pick up mercury? I have because I dropped this big thermometer once in Science. The Chemistry teacher never noticed because she was in the stock room at the time with Mr Bacon who'd just dropped in to have his epidiascope adjusted, so I tried to kick all the little bits and pieces behind me under Sarah Swille's work bench. It was terrible. There were all these little bits of stuff like those tiny silver balls you have to get into holes in those puzzles with glass over the top (the holes are usually in people's ears and noses and on the end of squirrels' tails and things), and the more I kicked at them, the more appeared. There were thousands of them all rolling around on the floor of the Science lab and I had to go crawling about under the benches and in between people's legs and schoolbags with this teaspoon trying to pick them up, and, every time I grabbed one, it'd just slither away under somebody's shoe or something.

Well, every time I pick up a great big wadge of spaghetti, it just goes slithering off the edge of the spoon and slurps straight back into the pan like a squadron of worms on ice skates. So, instead, I carry the pan across to the table and put the plates down flat and try tipping it out.

That's O.K. except that all the spaghetti wants to go on the same plate. When you stop in the middle to try and dollop some on another plate, the spaghetti's all in one big line like a long rubber waterfall and all the other person gets is half a teaspoonful of watered down tomato soup. We did Gravity once in Physics, but I can't remember what we decided about it. So, what I do now is lift up the plate with the spaghetti on and start pouring it back again. When half of it's back in the pan, I lift my arm higher and higher to try to stop the rest of it from falling off the plate. But I'm not tall enough, so I stand on the stool.

So here I am, standing on the stool with this plate of spaghetti, trying to manoeuvre the dangling ends within splash-down distance of the tomato sauce, when there's this knock on the door. I won't tell you what I say because I'm trying not to use any more bad language in this book, but I just don't see how people can be so stupid as to wait until you're dividing spaghetti out before they come and call for you.

I look around for somewhere to balance the plate of spaghetti but there isn't anywhere high enough (the spaghetti waterfall's grown to about four-foot-six by now), so I just carry on dangling and hope they'll give up and go away, but they don't. They keep on knocking.

In the end I try to compose my face to look as if I always receive visitors standing on a stool with my arms stretched up in the air dangling spaghetti on to the kitchen table, and I shout, 'Come in.'

It's a woman. A horrible woman with one of those plastic imitation leather coats on and a right enormous fur collar and blond hair that looks as if it's a wig and so much make-up that you can't even begin to work out what her face is like underneath. She looks foul.

'What do you want?' I ask her.

She stares at me as if she's never seen anybody serving spaghetti before. I hate being stared at. 'What are you doing?' she says.

Silly cow. What does it look like? I try to think of something stupid to say like I'm wall-papering the ceiling or working out new patterns in macramé or something, but she doesn't look the sort who'd appreciate a joke. I concentrate on the spaghetti instead, wriggling it about with the spoon to try and make it drop, and I don't say anything.

The woman is still looking at me, waiting for me to answer and, when she realizes that I can't be bothered explaining why I'm in the air, she asks, 'Does Mr O'Leary live here?'

I might have known. She's probably some girl friend that he's picked up down at the pub when he's been too drunk to see what she looked like. She's horrible. She's got no right to come round here.

I don't bother to look up. I just mumble, 'Yes,' under my breath and go and lose control over the spaghetti dish. Everything cascades over the edge all at once. Some of it lands on the other plate but most of it dollops on the table-cloth or on the floor, and it's all this woman's fault for staring at me. I wish her wig would fall off.

I'm not going to scrape the spaghetti up off the table-cloth and the floor and put it back on the plates whilst she's watching me, so I walk straight over and open the back door, waiting for her to go. 'He's not in,' I say. 'He's out.'

She looks sort of uncomfortable as if she doesn't know what to say, but I just stare at her. I'm positive now that it's a wig. It's a completely different colour from her eyebrows and you can see the place where it joins on, just above her ears. She's wearing long, fancy ear-rings as well. I hate long ear-rings.

'He's not in,' I say again a bit louder. I don't understand why he wants to have anything to do with women like her. Mum never would've worn a wig or piles of make-up or anything like that, and she always used to look really nice.

She still keeps hopping around a bit as if the elastic's just gone in her knickers. She looks a right mess. 'I thought . . . he was expecting me to come . . .' she starts off saying. Then, when she sees me still scowling at her, she changes her mind and turns to go outside. 'Never mind,' she says. 'I'll see him some other time.'

I don't even bother to say good-bye. I slam the door with my foot.

It's about twenty minutes later when my father comes home. He's looking all cheerful and jolly and he's wearing his new black leather jacket and a smart blue denim shirt that I don't think I've seen before. He's always wasting money. He's got these brown paper parcels under his arm, as well, *and* a bottle of wine. 'Hello, love,' he says, all smiles and charm. 'Had a nice day?'

He's probably been drinking. When he's had a lot to drink he's either ever so cheerful or ever so depressed or ever so sick. I don't say anything so he puts the parcels on the table and goes to take his coat off. While he's out of the room I take the spaghetti from the oven – that's where I'd put it after I'd scraped it off the floor – and stand it on the table. It looks revolting. It's like a pile of dried-up worms in cat's blood. I think I'll open a tin next time.

When he comes back in the kitchen and sees the spaghetti, he sort of stops dead in his tracks and you can see the smile actually drooping from his face. 'I didn't think you'd have made any tea yet,' he says, pointing at the brown paper parcels on the table. 'I called at the Chinese take-away. Do you think you could eat some?'

He looks at me with this pleading sort of smile he's got, so I say O.K. and start to take the food out of the bags. He's got me sweet and sour pork which is my favourite but I'm already full up with spaghetti. I might just manage a couple of mouthfuls.

'We're expecting a visitor, actually,' he says, picking up the bottle of wine.

I might have known. He wouldn't have brought food like that for us two, would he?

'Do you remember Mrs Kent?' he says, pulling out the cork and pouring us a glass of wine each.

'No.'

'She was in the bed next to your mother in the hospital, don't you remember? She was very good to your mother ... went to visit her later on ...' He starts piling all my mucky pans and things in the sink instead of sitting down and eating his tea. '... She had cancer of the throat ... and they managed to cure it. The thing I admired so much about her ...' He talks on and on when he's in this kind of mood as though there's somebody listening to him. '... was the way she made such an effort to talk to your mother and keep her spirits up. She was in terrible pain, you know. It really hurt her throat to speak after all that treatment, but she did such a lot to keep your mum feeling cheerful ...'

He comes across and sorts his cutlery out, not really wanting to start his tea when his visitor hasn't turned up yet. He just sits down then and drinks his wine. 'You do remember her, don't you?' he asks me.

I do actually, but I don't want him to know that. 'No,' I say and then I have a thought. 'What does she look like?' I ask him.

'Mmmmmm.' He smiles a bit as if he doesn't know where to start, '... well ... she was very different from your mum ... from how your mum *was*,' he corrects himself. 'A lot of make-up and so forth. And of course she lost nearly all her hair with the radium treatment ...'

I take a mouthful of wine and think how horrible it tastes. 'She's been already,' I tell him.

'What?'

'She came earlier on and went again.'

He looks a bit upset. 'What do you mean?' he asks me. 'Why didn't she stay and wait?'

I have another sip of wine and wait a second whilst I

swallow it. 'She said she wouldn't stop when she saw you weren't here. She said she might see you later on.'

I can see that he's looking at me in a flabbergasted sort of way, expecting me to explain things better. But I don't. I dive into the sweet and sour pork and ignore him as much as I can. It wasn't my fault. I didn't know that stupid woman was supposed to be coming for her tea. He should have told me. What does he think I am? A mind reader?

'I just happened to bump into her on my way to work this morning,' he still prattles on as though I'm looking interested, 'so I asked her round. I thought I could just call at the Chinese and be back before she got here.'

At last he starts unpacking his Chicken Chow Mein and looks as if he's going to eat something. He tries not to look at the spaghetti which is still welded together in front of him like the latest style in table decorations . . .

'It's new! It's terrific!
It's a dead worm table decoration!
Specially brought to you by . . .'

'There was a long queue at the take-away,' he tells me, but I keep my eyes on my sweet and sour pork and try to ignore him. As I was saying, none of it's my fault and I don't know why he cares. I wouldn't.

10

'Unhappy that I am, I cannot heave
My heart into my mouth.'

(Cordelia, Act I, Scene I)

'Lie in whichever position is most comfortable for you. You can stretch out on your back or curl up with your head under your arm . . . you know what suits you best. But choose a position where you can be really comfortable . . .'

I lie curled up in a ball in a corner of the room away from most of the others. I rest my head upon my folded arms and wait . . .

'. . . and now I want you to start relaxing your body . . . the way you've been taught . . . let your limbs start to sag and then go limp. Just let your body feel as though it's sinking through the floor . . .'

The room is very quiet so it's difficult to believe that there are twenty people here. The lights are dimmed down very low and there's no heating fan because the boiler room's next door. It's nice and comfy and quiet. You can forget that you're at school . . .

'Now, make sure that your muscles are relaxed . . . right up through your body. Concentrate on each part of your body in turn and try to feel as if you're completely weightless . . .' Miss Gloucester's walking round the room quietly between the laid out bodies. I can hear the padding of her bare feet on the floor as she passes near my face. '. . . Make sure that the muscles of your neck are completely relaxed . . . and your face . . . let your mouth relax . . . and your eyes . . .'

At first my muscles are tense and hard, as taut as tiny

apples, but then I make them relax, sinking my body into the silence. And I feel the darkness and the stillness wash over me like ripples on the edge of a lake. My mind goes blank. I feel myself drawn towards the darkness.

'Now, in the darkness of your mind, I want you to imagine a piece of blank white paper. Take a pencil, an imaginary pencil in your hand, and with that pencil I want you to draw on the paper some of the things that have happened to you recently. Write down what you can remember. The things that you've done. The things that people have said to you . . .'

I take the pencil, thinking hard.

'. . . concentrate in particular on things that people have said to annoy you or upset you . . . write them down . . . write them on the paper . . .'

I start to write. There are lots of things to remember.

'. . . any things that people have said or done to make you angry or to hurt you . . . write them down . . . write them on the paper. Think hard. Don't miss anything out.'

I start at the top of the paper and work downwards, filling all the spaces in with things that have happened to me.

'You should be completely relaxed now and you're writing on the paper all the things that have happened to you . . . all the upsetting things . . .'

My thumb and first finger are squeezed together with the pencil, scribbling away. There's so much to write and I've got to find room on the paper. Filling all the corners up, turning the paper round and writing down the edges . . .

'You'll have to write quickly now. You don't have very much time left . . . write anything else down . . . on the paper . . . anything else you can remember . . .' Miss Gloucester keeps walking round the room and her voice comes nearer and goes away again. I scribble away still in the corners, trying to get the writing finished. It's very important to me that I fill the paper up.

'Now, I want you to finish what you're writing and rest for a moment. Let your hand relax . . . Look at the paper in front of you, filled with writing. The paper's full. There's no room now for anything else.

'And I want you to pick up with your hand a big eraser . . . imagine a great big rubber in your hand . . . look carefully at the paper and, starting anywhere you like, begin to rub out what you've written. Press hard because the writing's very firm and strong. Start to rub out . . . anywhere you like . . . start erasing now . . .'

I start at the corners of the paper, reading what I've written. Rubbing it out.

SCHOOL IS FOUL.

I HATE SCHOOL.

I HATE ENGLISH.

ALL TEACHERS PICK ON ME.

'Remember you have to press very hard . . . deep down on the paper. Rub it out. Don't leave anything . . .'

I press hard, whitening my knuckles with the tension.

I WAS LATE FOR DINNER AND I
MISSED DARREN.
IT'S ALL SNORTALOTTE'S FAULT.

Pressing down hard on to the floor with my fingers . . .

'Come on now, press down hard. Obliterate everything. All the hatred and the tension. Rub it out . . . get rid of it all . . . scratch everything out . . . scratch it hard . . .'

I DIDN'T WANT TO COME TO SCHOOL TODAY. I HATE SCHOOL. THERE'S NOWHERE ELSE TO GO.

MY FATHER WOULDN'T COME AND TELL THEM TO STOP PICKING ON ME. HE WOULDN'T EVEN GIVE ME A CHANCE TO ASK HIM.

I CAN'T STAND MY FATHER.

My finger-nails scraping on the wooden floor . . .

I HATE – – –

I HATE – – –

. . . scratching it out. Pressing down hard . . .

I HATE MY FATHER!!!

I WANT TO KILL HIM!!!

'Right, now you remember the point we'd reached yesterday . . .'

We're all sitting round in a semicircle again and Miss Gloucester pauses a moment with her hand across her eyes as though she's thinking. She wraps her long skirt round her legs and tucks her bare feet inside it. It's not hard to remember what we were doing yesterday although, like I say, I thought most of it seemed very strange.

'Lear had a third daughter,' Miss Gloucester goes on, 'his youngest daughter, Cordelia, who seems to have been his favourite. Rebecca . . .' she looks up suddenly and fixes her eyes upon me . . . 'will you please play Cordelia?'

Oh no. I get that awful feeling of dread inside me again. Usually I'm very pleased if I get chosen for anything in Drama, but today I just feel worried. I don't see how I'm going to play this part . . .

'. . . and Darren, Darren Edmunds . . . will you please take the part of Lear?'

I don't know what to think. I feel excited because I'm playing opposite Darren, but I'm sure I'm going to make a fool of myself.

'Take your time,' Miss Gloucester's saying. 'Just try and feel your way into the part and start as soon as you're ready.'

I still don't know what to do. I just stand there looking over at Darren on the other side of the room as if I'm expecting him to leap across and rescue me and show me what to do. But of course he doesn't. First of all he smiles at me and then, whilst I'm still picking myself up from the floor like a melted ice cube, he strides across to sit down on the stool and I can see that he's getting himself into the part straightaway and expecting me to do the same.

Darren lifts up the black cloak that Miss Gloucester's left out and he throws it around his shoulders, but he doesn't bother with the cardboard crown. He doesn't need it. He looks just like a king. You can tell by the way that he sits and lifts up his head that he's making himself feel strong and powerful.

I still feel all peculiar and liquified like an ice-cream cornet in a heat wave. I stare at the floor and clasp my hands together so that nobody can see how much they're shaking.

'Well?' Darren's voice is strong and forceful. It echoes round the hall. 'Your sisters have spoken.'

I know he's staring at me. Hard. And so is everyone else in the room, but I still don't say anything. I just glare down at the floor in front of me and wish that I was beautiful and clever and proud of myself.

'Your sisters have expressed their feelings for me,' he goes on. 'Now it's your turn . . .'

The silence is warm and heavy as everyone looks at me, waiting for an answer. It's not fair. With anyone else I think I could have acted – just made up any old thing to please them, but with Darren it's different. I can't tell him like this in public with everybody watching. I can't just say how much I love him. It's not right. I look down at the toes of my plimsolls. The others start shuffling around as though they're feeling a bit impatient.

'Have you nothing to say. . . ?' asks Darren and his voice is starting to get angry now as if he's tired of being kept waiting.

I force myself to look up at him. I'm feeling angry now as well because I don't think I should have to do this. You shouldn't have to tell somebody how much you fancy them in front of a whole room full of people. I feel like running into a corner and sitting down and hiding, but I really do want to be in this play and I think I've made enough of a fool of myself already.

I lift up my head and stare Darren straight between the eyes. He's got lovely eyes. I take a deep breath and say the first thing that comes into my head. 'I love you just as much as you deserve,' I tell him. I say it straight out without stammering or anything, and without really thinking what it means.

He looks taken aback a bit. 'Is that all?' he asks me.

'I just have the feelings that you'd expect a daughter to have for her father,' I tell him. I think that's very clever of me because it means different things to different people.

'Is that all you can say?' he asks me again and this time his voice is getting louder and stronger.

'Yes,' I say.

His eyes are flashing with anger and he looks really annoyed now. He's gorgeous when he's mad.

Suddenly Miss Gloucester stands up and comes across to interrupt. 'Thank you very much,' she says. 'That was excellent – both of you. You really got into the parts . . . I'm sorry we don't have time for any more.'

I feel a rush of pleasure. Nobody ever pays me a compliment normally so it's really nice when somebody says something good about me. But I still feel very puzzled. I didn't say anything at all like the other daughters did so I don't see how I can have said it right.

I smile across at Darren and he grins and walks over. He puts his hand on my arm for a fraction of a second and I feel as if I'm on a roller coaster. Right at the top. 'You were very good,' he says. He smiles at me again and we sit down in the circle. Next to each other.

11

'I grow, I prosper;
Now, gods, stand up for bastards!'
(Edmund, Act I, Scene II)

It's Tuesday. And today I'm supposed to be writing about what happened at the week-end, but I'm not going to tell you about it because it was too horrible.

If you remember, I was going to have this perm done on Saturday and then I was going to the youth club disco on Saturday night because that's where Darren goes. And you'll probably remember that I had my money stolen. I haven't forgotten anyway. So I couldn't have the perm.

But I did go to the disco. I washed my hair and set it myself. It didn't look right exciting but it was O.K. And then I just can't bring myself to tell you what happened when I got to the youth club. I'm sorry but it hurts me too much to even think about it. I meant to write everything down that had happened when I started writing this book, but some things are just too painful. It was absolutely horrible and I've never felt so sorry for myself in my life as I do just now, so you'll have to excuse me; I'm sorry.

That's why this chapter is so short.

12

'Let's exchange charity.
I am no less in blood than thou art, Edmund;
If more, the more thou hast wrong'd me.'

(Edgar, Act V, Scene III)

On Monday morning I didn't go to school. I couldn't face it. I told my father that I had a stomachache when he came to ask me why I hadn't got up and then I turned over and went straight back to sleep. He brought me a cup of tea later on but I didn't drink it. He makes horrible tea, anyway.

I didn't want to get to school before dinner-time, because I couldn't face going to Drama and I knew I couldn't bear it if anybody asked me why I hadn't been. Not that anybody would be bothered, but I could never tell them. I hate Darren Edmunds. I hate him more than anybody else in the whole wide world. I wish his . . . Well, I won't tell you what particular part of Darren Edmunds' anatomy I want to drop off. I'll leave that to your imagination.

I went to school for a couple of hours in the afternoon but I couldn't really cope with it. I couldn't settle. I never did any work.

And it was the same in the evening. I was walking up and down, changing channels every couple of minutes on the television, then looking out of the window and then switching the radio on and off. And after that this noise kept getting on my nerves. It's stupid really. It's not easy to explain about it when you write it down. It just sounds silly. But all of a sudden I couldn't stand the noise the clock was making. You know, ticking. It wasn't as if it jumped up and growled at me or something; it was just ticking away like it usually does but it seemed to get louder. I know this sounds stupid but that's what really happened. The ticking on the clock seemed to get louder and louder and louder so it was echoing around inside my head. *Tick-tock, tick-tock, tick-tock,* as if it was taking over everything. Taking over the world. It was terrifying. I couldn't stand it. I squeezed my hands over my ears and lay down on the settee with a big cushion on my head but, do you know, after a few minutes I still could hear it. Getting louder again, *tick-tock, tick-tock, tick-tock*.

I wanted to scream. I really did. I wanted to scream and tear my hair out, and I writhed about as if I was in agony. I squeezed my hands tighter and tighter over my ears and rolled about but then, every time I was still, I heard the noise again, echoing round like a time bomb: *tick-tock, tick-tock, tick-tock*.

I ran upstairs. I ran into my bedroom and slammed the door. Then I threw myself down on the bed with the pillow round my head and hammered my fist on the mattress. After that I lay still for a moment. Listening. I strained my ears until they hurt me, listening for some silence, but all that I could hear was noise and more noise. First of all I heard the springs in the mattress through my head, squeaking back into shape. Then a dog kept barking. After that there were some kids outside on the street, playing football or something, and you could hear them shouting to each other and the sound of their ball bouncing on the road, *bounce, bounce, booiing!* I wanted to strangle them. I couldn't stand it.

I wrapped the pillow round my head again as if I was in pain and I rolled about, rocking from side to side on the bed, screaming silently and plugging my mouth with the pillowcase. 'Help me!' I screamed inside my head. 'Help me!' And then, because I didn't know what else to shout, 'Please, God . . . please, please help me!' And I thought for a couple of seconds of the God that my mother had told me about who lives like a spirit inside people. I tried to imagine what He was like and how you could talk to Him, but I couldn't. I don't know how you talk to spirits. 'Please, God, help me!' I screamed at Him again inside my head, just in case He was listening, but I didn't think He was.

And then I rolled and writhed around the bed some more, banging my fists down on to the mattress and the pillow and scraping my fingers down the walls. I don't like telling you about all this because, like I say, it sounds so stupid, but this was what I did on Monday night. I didn't cry or anything; I just screamed inside my head and after a bit I fell asleep. I had all my clothes on and downstairs I'd left the gas fire on in the front room and the light as well but I just fell asleep without thinking about it and got up in the middle of the night and put my nightie on. It was very strange. I felt frightened of myself.

And now it's Tuesday and I'm on my way to school. It's funny how you can't ever bring a note to say that you were just too sad to come to school; you have to make something up about stomachaches and headaches and things. And, although I feel better today than I did last night, I still feel strange. I feel as though inside me there's something foul and obnoxious bubbling away and I've got to keep it from escaping. It's horrible and frightening. Like a steaming volcano of poisonous slime that I've got to try to keep in check. Any minute now it's going to escape and start bubbling over and exploding.

I don't want to talk to anybody. I walk to school early to be sure I'm by myself because I couldn't bear it if somebody came and spoke to me. I think I'd just burst into tears.

I'm doing all right, walking along the road all by myself, until I see this dead mouse lying on the pavement. I don't know how I'd normally react, but today I just stop, completely still, and stare at it, absolutely horrified. I feel sick. Really sick. And, although it sounds silly to say this, I feel as though somebody actually came and put this dead mouse here just to upset me when I walked past. It's horrible.

Like I say, I wasn't feeling too good when I set off this morning and I'm feeling even worse now. I feel sort of shaky and giddy, so I just go and stand in the doorway of Horace Oglet's shop for a few minutes and stare at the black pudding and polony as though they're the nicest things I've seen all week whilst I recover. Then I take a few deep breaths and I make myself set off again before the crowd starts growing.

At school I do my best to keep out of everybody's way, and in English I even go and sit by myself in the desk right at the front next to where Mr Bacon sits. It mixes him up then because he hasn't got a place for people to sit when they've been talking. I even do some work. That shows how sick I am. I do a list of words and their opposites and write them in a sentence *and* I get them right. That just goes to show you how strangely I'm behaving.

I see Darren in the dining-hall, and when I see him I take my tray right over to the other side of the room and sit at a table on my own and I scowl at anybody who tries to sit next to me. I think carefully about going to Drama. I really don't want to go again because I couldn't stand working with Darren in a group or anything but, on the other hand, why should I let him spoil everything for me? It's not fair. I want to be in the play. I like acting. I've got every right to go if I want to. If I stay away from Drama, that'll just be another thing that Darren's fouled up for me, and why should I let him mess up my life?

I walk around for a few minutes after dinner still deciding what to do, but I'm plagued by people like Cynthia Snort grunting at me to make me go outside and by people trying to tell me bits of boring gossip that nobody wants to hear. So in the end I fetch my clothes and go down to the Drama Workshop.

The Relaxation's terrible. I can no more relax than balance a warthog on my nose. I just lie there in a knot, huddled in a corner in the dark, tense as a tiger, wound up like a clockwork Womble. When we sit up and open our eyes, Miss Gloucester talks about what everyone did on Monday and I realize that I've missed out again. It's not easy to follow this play.

'The situation now', she says, 'is where Lear goes to visit his daughter. Try to imagine how they feel . . .' She turns around and faces me. 'Rebecca,' she says, 'will you please play Regan today . . .? And Darren, will you take Lear? You were both doing so well last time . . .'

I don't say anything. I can't explain why, but it just seems like Fate that I've been chosen, as though it *had* to happen. As though what took place on Saturday night had to finish today with the two of us here in Drama, standing face to face. It's just as though this is the thing I've been waiting for all day without realizing it.

I stand up straightaway and walk into the centre of the room and wait for Darren. He gets up slowly, taken aback, as if he doesn't know what's going to happen. I do. I stare at him and he lowers his eyes to the floor as he walks across the room.

I keep on glaring at him as he stands in front of me with his head bowed down, waiting. 'What do you want?' I sneer at him. And as he stands there, still looking downwards at his feet, I suddenly notice how ugly he looks. He's horrible.

I think he must have expected me to talk to him all nicely, all lovey-dovey, because he's supposed to be my father, and he looks put out and hurt. I'm glad. I think of what he did on Saturday and I don't mind hurting him. 'I asked you what you've come here for,' I snarl at him before he's got chance to compose himself again.

He squirms and rubs his hands together. 'I . . . er . . .' He looks up at me with that pleading sort of smile. Just like my father's got. 'I've . . . er . . . I've come to stay with you . . .'

'You what!'

'I've come to stay here.'

He takes a step forward and reaches out to touch me on my arm, but I jump back in horror and brush his arm away as if it's a dead slug. He looks up at me and I can see he's determined to get round me somehow or other. Now he's trying to switch on the charm. Some hope.

'Get lost.'

'Come on, love,' he says, smiling at me as he reaches forward again to touch my hand. 'It's all right.'

My stomach turns over and I feel my knees starting to tremble. I'm almost ready to give way. *Come on, love . . .* The sound of his voice when he makes it gentle like that, it brings back everything that happened: him whispering in the darkness, his lips touching my ear . . . me, melting, softening like a week-old puppy . . . *Come on, love. It's all right*. His voice like music to me, and me with my arms around his neck, wanting to please him . . . wishing I wasn't so scared . . . wondering what to say . . .

'Come on . . .'

I want to scream. I hate him. 'Don't you dare touch me!' I yell at him, pulling my hand away so quickly I nearly knock him over. I feel the volcano inside me starting to bubble over. The poisonous slime's escaping. 'Who do you think you are?' I shout at him. 'What right have you got to come and talk to me like that?'

He opens his mouth and starts to speak. He stutters a bit so I don't even give him chance.

'You bastard!' I shriek at him. 'Get out of my life! Leave me alone!'

'You don't know what you're saying, Regan . . .' He's really getting upset now. 'That's no way to talk to . . .'

'Don't you *dare* speak to me again. Ever.'

'You've no right to . . .'

'You bastard! You horrible stinking bastard!'

He looks bewildered and taken aback. He doesn't know what to do. He glances round at the circle of faces in the hall and at Miss Gloucester, as if one of them could help him. Everyone's just staring. Waiting. I feel the blood pounding through my head. I'm panting and out of breath with the exertion of screaming at him.

Slowly he looks up and speaks to me, deliberately pressing his words with hurt and malice. 'You . . . ungrateful . . . child!' he says. And it sounds effective because it's low and loaded and a contrast to my shouting. 'You ungrateful child . . .'

But I won't give in. I think about walking back into the crowded room afterwards on Saturday. The noise and heavy air. I think about him walking off and leaving me. As though it didn't matter. I think about him putting his arm round that other girl and dancing with her. Making sure that I was watching. I think of myself walking home in the dark. Alone. I hate him. I don't have to shout. I can load my voice as well. Smother it with resentment. 'I think you are foul and despicable,' I say. 'I want nothing more to do with you.' I'm speaking slowly now, easing out the remnants of the hatred, drop by drop. 'I never want to speak to you again. I never want you near my house. I hate you.'

I walk back across the room, calmly to my place, leaving him speechless and open-mouthed in the middle of the room. I'm not even shaking. I even feel calm and composed. The room is deathly silent. I sit down.

13

'Love, and be silent . . .'

(Cordelia, Act I, Scene I)

I expect people to say something to me about what happened in Drama but they don't. I think they don't know what to say. People keep away from me as if I've got something infectious, like leprosy. As if I'm not safe to be near. I even think they might be afraid of me, but if they are I'm not surprised. I feel afraid of myself sometimes.

I've got through yet another day without Miss Hoggit sending for me. I'm beginning to wonder if she's avoiding me. Teachers don't exactly queue up nowadays to come and talk to me. They're probably drawing lots in the back of the staff-room to decide who's going to tell me off. I'll probably get a letter one day:

'Dear Rebecca,
You have been expelled . . .'

Perhaps they're writing it now. You never know with teachers.

When I get home from school, I feel a lot calmer and I decide to do something else unusual. I decide to do some homework. I couldn't stand any of the teachers going mad at me this week; lessons are bad enough as it is. I've missed the last two English homeworks and Mr Bacon'll have hysterics if I miss this one as well. I can just imagine him, turning purple, glowering over me with his hair standing on end and steam escaping from his nostrils.

We've got to write a story about smugglers. It's all to do with this idiotic book we're reading about smugglers in . . . I don't know, the twenty-first century B.C., I think it is. Whenever it is, it's rubbish. Streaky – that's Mr Bacon (in case you hadn't guessed) – said that we could write about modern day smugglers if we wanted to – he said that as if he was doing us a really big favour – and all the posh kids in our class started showing off about going through Customs at airports and hoverports and things like that. I've never even been abroad, so you can just imagine how easy it's going to be for me to write this story.

I haven't much energy tonight so I sit down in an armchair and switch on this old King Kong film on the television to help me think whilst I'm writing. I like King Kong. And when it gets to the part where they've captured him and they're taking him off to America, all of a sudden this relates to the story I've got to write. Because one thing I notice is that they don't take King Kong through the Customs. The man who wrote the film just cheats and misses that part out altogether, and I decide that what would make a really good story about smugglers would be the conversation when they try to smuggle King Kong through the Customs. I'm not having him going to New York because I'm not sure what sort of things they'd say in America.

It's quite a good story. King Kong is so massive that when he walks through the Customs all that anybody can see of him is his hairy legs, and the people trying to get him out of the country pretend it's a special black hairy carpet made out of yak skin all rolled up. When the Customs official starts getting awkward and asking too many difficult questions, King Kong stamps on him and all the Customs hall gets squashed. It's a very good plot. *I* like it anyway.

I feel a bit happier when I go upstairs to bed because I

think I've written something good. Streaky Bacon'll probably say that it's stupid, but I don't care. He always reads out Amelia Hamlet's stories, or Sarah Swille's, and he says mine are rubbish. Mind you, I usually write them as I'm walking down the corridor on my way to the lesson, so they're never all that brilliant.

Before I go to bed, I open my money-box and have a look inside in case the money's come back yet, but it hasn't. I've looked inside it every day since last Wednesday and there's not so much as a half p. extra. I don't know what to do. I know I ought to mention it but I can't bring myself to discuss anything as personal as that with him. I can't bring myself to discuss anything with him at all, so what hope is there?

When I get into bed I still feel calm. I don't want to bang my head on the wall or scream or anything like that. I think back to last night when I screamed out in my head for God to help me and I wonder if it worked. I don't see how it can have, but I do need all the help I can get and there aren't a lot of other people around at the moment that I can turn to.

As I lie there in my bed, I try to empty my mind and feel the Silence – the way my mother tried to teach me when I was little. It isn't easy. I have to grope around in the darkness, forcing my way forward between all these images in my mind and all of them are hostile and threatening and jostling for space in my head. I can see a picture of my money-box with the lid off and then the dead mouse. I see Darren's eyes filled with anger, and then he's at the youth club with his arm around that horrible girl. I see my father being sick in the garden and King Kong's massive foot stomping down on to masses of people. I concentrate hard and try to push them all aside; frowning and tense, I try to squeeze out the darkness between them. It's no good.

I take a deep breath and relax. For a fraction of a second

the images clear and then . . . whilst my mind is in this half-way stage suspended in between thoughts, the Silence comes. Silence isn't really the word to describe what I mean because it isn't like the emptiness of a vacuum. It isn't just a big gap. It's a sort of silent surging that makes your whole body vibrate. It's like a sort of peace, but it's fantastically exciting as well. It's not easy to describe, but I heard somebody say once, 'The Peace of God which Passeth all Understanding', and that's what it's like. You can't cling on to it and keep it because in a few seconds it's all over and finished, but I know that it's been through me. It's a bit frightening as well. Because I feel as though what I've just had a tiny glimpse of is something powerful and massive – like finding King Kong's footprint in the mud. Only bigger. And nicer. I don't know what to think now. I lie in the darkness, struggling to recapture the Silence and the Peace of God which Passeth all Understanding, but I try too hard and it makes me miss it. Whilst I'm still trying, I fall asleep.

In my dream I'm in a castle, a big, old, wooden castle. I look out of the window and see this figure galloping along on horseback with a huge standard in his hand. I go downstairs to meet him.

When I arrive at the door, for some strange reason, instead of going out to meet the horseman, I start fastening the door up and bolting it. Locking him out. I didn't mean to do that when I came downstairs at first – I must have changed my mind. I spend ages messing about with the heavy bolts and locks on this great big wooden door and when I finally get it all fastened, I hear noises scuffling behind me and I realize that someone else has gone to smuggle the horseman into the castle through the back door. It's been a right waste of time. I walk down the darkened passageway to see what's happening at the back of the castle and then, in the middle of the passageway, I find my way blocked by this enormous tree trunk. It's growing right in the middle of the castle and it's black and hairy. I look up. It goes higher and higher . . . towering about two hundred feet above me.

I look upwards in the sky to find its branches and instead I see two long hairy arms swinging down, black and muscular. Right at the very top I see this head, bending down and leering at me. With horror I realize that I'm looking at a face I recognize: Darren Edmunds. Darren Edmunds plays King Kong.

14

'Things that love night
Love not such nights as these; the wrathful skies
Gallow the very wanderers of the dark . . .'

(Kent, Act III, Scene II)

'Now today I want us to explore the idea of rejection . . .' Miss Gloucester wraps her long Indian skirt around her knees as she sits cross-legged in front of us. She blinks and rubs her eyes. 'Would anyone like to explain, first of all, what it means? What are we thinking about when we use the word "rejection"?'

There's a pause for a minute while all the brainy kids in the Group think about it.

'It's . . . like . . . when nobody wants you,' Bernice Berkshire suggests. I don't know what she knows about it. She's got more lads running after her than a champion long-distance runner.

'Yes . . .' says Miss Gloucester, blinking again and rubbing her eyes with the back of her hand.

'They have rejects at a factory,' chirrups Timothy Trotter. 'Like things they don't want. Things that's not come out right . . .'

'Yeah. You buy 'em cheap at the sales.'

'That's right,' says Jonathan. 'My mum bought some tights once and when she got 'em home she found they'd only got one leg . . .'

'They'd be right rejects, then . . .'

'Yeah. Like you.' A few people laugh at this, but it isn't really funny.

'We bought a pork pie once with a piglet's eyeball in it . . .'

'Don't be daft,' says Timothy Trotter. 'They're hard boiled eggs they put in the middle.'

'No, it wasn't. It was a proper piglet's eyeball. My mum took it to the 'ealth inspector . . .'

Miss Gloucester pulls a face when she hears about the eyeball and then she sits, patiently, waiting to get back to the subject.

'Can you think of any other examples', she says, when everybody's calmed down and stopped nattering, 'of occasions when people might *feel* rejected – the way King Lear did?'

This makes me cringe. I'm always feeling rejected but I wouldn't want to talk about it. I think about Darren and I think about my father; I think about teachers at school. I hope she doesn't ask me.

'If you audition for a part in a play or something and people tell you that you're not good enough . . . then you feel rejected.' That's Bernice Berkshire again. Like I say, she's always talking about things she knows nothing about. She'd never miss getting a part in anything. She's had more parts than a Build-yourself-a-Jumbo-Jet-out-of-Legobricks kit.

'Like when you go in for the trials for a team or something and then you don't get selected . . .' Timothy Trotter knows all about that. He once told us how he went in the trials for St Cuthbert's Tiddleywinks Tournament. They didn't actually tell him he was no good – just asked him if he would mind being the tea masher instead. He's never been very good at sport.

'You might get invited to a party and when you get there people say, "What've you come for?" You know – as if they don't want you . . .'

'Your boy friend goes off with your best mate . . .'

'You get turned down for a job you've just had an interview for . . .'

Everybody knows what it means. They've all got plenty to say about it anyway. But, as I sit cross-legged on the floor and listen to them all chattering away, it seems as though I'm the only one who really understands what rejection's all about. The other kids are wanted and looked after, with nice mums and dads who think they're wonderful and boy friends or girl friends who think they're marvellous and teachers who never pick on them. They've got people who like them even when they're horrible. Nobody likes me. Even when I'm nice.

'So what I want you to do now is split up into pairs and try to work out a scene . . . an encounter of some kind . . . where one of you will feel completely rejected. You can use some of the ideas we've been talking about or work out some more of your own . . . it's up to you. So will you each find yourself a partner . . . ?'

I don't really want to have any part in this. I feel rejected enough with just being me, without having to dress up as a one-legged pair of tights or a pork pie with a piglet's eyeball in the middle. I creep away into a corner whilst everybody's choosing partners and hope that no one'll notice me. With any luck I'll be able to just sit out and watch.

Everybody's sorted themselves out and are busy discussing what scene they're going to do, when Miss Gloucester walks across. 'I think we'll have to work together,' she says, as though it's everybody else's fault that she's been left on her own. 'Have you got any ideas?' she asks me.

'No.'

'What about something one of the others has suggested?'

'I don't think I could do any of those.'

'Wasn't there anything that appealed to you?'

'No.'

We sit in silence for a moment or two watching the other kids settling down to work. Then Miss Gloucester says, 'I know . . . I could be a drama teacher who's trying to think of all sorts of suggestions to help you understand this difficult play that we're doing, and every time I come up with an idea, you could just say, "Oh no, I don't like that," and then I'd feel rejected.'

She says the first part of this with a completely straight face so I don't realize that she's having me on, then she turns round and grins at me and I smile. I would never have thought of Miss Gloucester feeling rejected. You forget that teachers are people. I try to think of something quick. 'I know,' I tell her, 'let's pretend I've got nowhere to stay . . . I'm a woman that's left her husband because he's been bashing her about and you can be my sister or somebody I've come to see . . . some relation I've come to stay with . . .'

At least it doesn't sound too much like me. I can't imagine myself ever having a husband – not even one that bashed me about. The way that things are going I don't think I'll ever even have a proper boy friend.

'What time of day is it?' Miss Gloucester asks me.

'Night-time – two o'clock in the morning.'

'And you're going to be my sister?'

'Yes. Younger sister.'

I'm still not too keen on this but I act as if I'm carrying a little baby in my arms and come knocking on the door at Miss Gloucester's house and then, when she opens it, I sob out this terrible story about my husband and all the foul things he's been doing to me. I keep dabbing my eyes as if I'm crying and all the while keep rocking this imaginary baby. I make up quite a good story. I feel genuinely sorry when she won't allow me in the house. The baby's woken up and started crying. My arms are aching from the weight of carrying it.

''Orace 'asn't been well,' she moans at me, 'an' he's got to go in to work in the mornin'. You don't know what it's like when you've a business to run. The baby'd wake 'im up.'

'But she'll soon drop off to sleep again when I get her in a bed . . .'

'An' she'll be pickin' germs up. I don't know what it is that 'Orace has got, but I'm sure it's catchin'. I keep coming over funny myself.'

'But look, it's raining . . .' I know all this is just a story she's making up to get rid of me. '. . . it's starting to thunder as well; there'll be a right storm soon . . .'

'It's no good. You belong with yer 'usband; not with us.'

I feel hurt. 'I don't want to go back,' I say.

'I warned you not to marry 'im.'

'But . . .' I feel really upset. I'm getting soaked to the skin out here in the thunderstorm and the baby's writhing about now, screaming. I can hardly hold it. '. . . I'm your sister!' I shout at her. 'Your own flesh and blood.'

'So what?' she snarls. The stuck-up bitch. 'I've got me own family to look after an' so 'ave you. Now, get off 'ome.'

I don't know what to say. I stand there staring at her, dumb with disbelief. I don't know how anybody can be so cruel to a member of their own family. I don't know how they can be so horrible.

I sit on the floor with the baby in my lap. I pull up my knees so I'm curled up like a baby racoon in a nest and rock myself gently backwards and forwards, moaning softly. Rocking my baby and rocking myself, moaning and whimpering. My eyes are closed . . . there's no one in the world that loves me ... there's nobody to care about me ... the well of loneliness starts to creep back through the air holes in my mind ... I think I want to die ...

15

'Winter's not gone yet, if the wild-geese fly that way.'

(Fool, Act II, Scene IV)

The next morning I decide I can't cope again and I go to school late. It's after dinner when I arrive. At afternoon break, when I see Bernice Berkshire, I decide to ask her if she'd mind lending me her copy of *King Lear*. Then I can have a look through and try to understand the play a bit better.

'Did you go to Drama at dinner-time?' I ask her.

'No,' she says. 'It wasn't on. Why? What happened to you?'

'I didn't come in till this afternoon.'

'Oh.' She hands her packet of Porkypeeces out to me and I help myself. They're like crisps only shaped like piglets and made out of chemicals and flavouring. They don't taste too bad, considering.

'Haven't you heard about Miss Gloucester, then?' Bernice asks me, her mouth crammed full of synthetic piglets.

'No. What about her?'

'She's had to go into hospital. Miss Hoggit told us this morning in Assembly that there wouldn't be a drama practice today and, when I asked her about it at break, she said that Miss Gloucester had had to go into hospital.'

'Did she say what was the matter with her?'

'Something called a cataract.'

I've never heard of anybody having that before. 'What's that mean?' I ask her.

'Something to do with her waterworks, I suppose.'

'That sounds painful.' Then I think about the play and

how well we're getting on with it. 'I was going to ask if I could borrow your *King Lear*,' I tell her, 'but we might not be doing it now . . . What do you think?'

'I don't know.' Bernice finishes the last of the Porky-peeces, screws up the empty packet in her fist and throws it in the direction of the rubbish bin. 'No,' she says, looking fed up. 'I don't know what we'll do about it now.'

I walk straight into the Meeting House and sit down on my own on the back corner of the bench seat. The room is very still. The chairs are set out in circles, all facing a table in the centre of the room. There are flowers on the table and some books. Nothing else really. The walls are just plain brick.

Outside, you can hear the sound of traffic and people passing by. You can hear the bells ringing at the Cathedral round the corner, but it sounds a long way off. In here it's quiet. Nobody speaks. People who come into the Meeting late creep soundlessly to places at the back. Everybody settles down. The loudest noise is the sound of people breathing.

Very soon, I feel the Silence. It's heavy and soft and it spreads and rises across the Meeting. It surges through me and presses upon my consciousness like a vision. A vision of Peace. It makes me feel very humble. And I sit in a kind of self-surrender. Absorbing sensations. Wallowing. Breathing in this power that's surging through me. I feel at peace.

And I feel the Silence in me. As the snow is in the snow-drift and the water is in the wave and the sap is in the tree . . . I close my eyes.

Minutes pass. I become aware of a movement nearby and someone rises. She begins to speak, quietly and calmly. And then she reads a passage from the Bible – one of the Psalms. Her voice echoes gently across the Meeting:

'God is our refuge and strength, a very present help in trouble . . .'

And I know that she is saying the words to me. The words reach me and are absorbed inside me. They were written for me . . .

'Therefore will not we fear, though the earth be removed, and though the mountains be carried into the midst of the sea . . .'

And I think of how afraid I used to be. How terribly lonely and afraid. And an unseen, gentle hand just wipes out the fears from my mind as thoroughly as blackened slush is thrust aside by the snow plough. And only the Peace is left. As white as fresh-fallen snow. Like an empty sheet of white paper . . .

'All the hatred and the tension. Rub it out . . . get rid of it all . . . scratch everything out . . . scratch it hard . . .' Just the plain white paper left. Empty at last. The white Peace.

'He maketh wars to cease unto the end of the earth; he breaketh the bow, and cutteth the spear in sunder; he burneth the chariot in the fire.

'Be still and know that I am God . . .'

I think at last I know. It's taken a long long time and it's not been easy. But I think I know at last. I think I've found the Stillness . . .

When the Meeting is over, the Clerk reads out the notices and then a man comes in with a trolley full of coffee cups. I take a cup and walk into the hallway to look at the notice board out there. There are petitions for people to sign about the arms trade and a notice about an anti-nuclear rally. Then there's some ideas for raising money to help Oxfam, but the main thing that takes my eye is a notice about a drama group. I won't ask anybody about it yet, I decide, but I might do later on, especially if Miss Gloucester has to stay in hospital so long that we can't finish the play.

I had a thought about Miss Gloucester whilst I was in the Meeting. That's one of the things about Quaker Meetings, you get these really good ideas suddenly springing from nowhere inside your head. I thought I could organize a whip-round at school from all the people in the Drama Workshop. Then some of us could go and visit her in hospital and take her a present and a card.

When my mum first went in the hospital, I bought her a sort of garden. A garden-in-a-bowl. It was really nice because the flowers didn't die the way they do when you just take a bunch of them to the hospital. They grew and grew all over the place, so Mum had to take a lot of cuttings off them when she came home. It cost more than a bunch of flowers, of course, but it was worth it.

I don't stay long at the Meeting House because I know that people will want to come and talk to me if they recognize who I am. Nobody is sure at first because I'm so much bigger now. I feel a bit embarrassed because I haven't been to a Meeting since I was in the children's group. I will talk to them, but later on. When I come another time.

At school on Monday morning I start looking for people from the Drama Workshop to ask about the money for Miss Gloucester. I haven't got a tin or anything, so I've brought my special money-box to school. I see a couple of people before Assembly starts and they promise to bring their money tomorrow.

After Assembly, Gertie Runt stands up and talks about some stupid trip to France she's organizing for people in the fourth and fifth years and says how people have to bring the money on Tuesday if they want to go. It makes me mad. If everybody's bringing cash to go bombing off to France with, I don't know how they'll remember 20p for my Miss Gloucester box. That's just typical of Gertie Runt.

The first lesson on Monday is English and Mr Bacon

says he's going to read out some of the best stories from last week. Some of the brainy kids start whispering, 'Mine's rubbish,' and 'Ooh, I hope he doesn't read mine out,' which means that really they think their story's fantastic and they're dying for him to read it out to the rest of the class.

I don't say anything. I stand my money-box up in front of me on the desk to give me something to look at whilst Streaky takes Sarah Swille's book from the top of the pile and starts reading out her story. She always gets her work read out, but really I don't think it's all that good. Whilst I'm listening, I stroke the painted figures on the box with my finger: the painted cat, the painted man and painted lady and I look at them carefully. I decide to write about them in the back of my French book – you're not allowed to use your English book for things like that. This is what I write:

SWISS CHALET

The painted cat, the painted people,
standing, staring, never changing;
their hollow smiles as fixed as fossils;
their minds as dry as deserts.
Their eyes stare tirelessly
but they see nothing.
They feel only the vibration of
wood as it ages;
they hear only their paint slowly cracking through
the centuries;
the timber soundlessly shrinking.
They feel no pain, no heartbreak.
They never cry and never laugh.
They stand as safe as starlight and
they love like androids in
a vacuum.

It's not brilliant, but it's a lot better than Sarah Swille's story that Streaky's still raving on about. I look at the figures again and try to think of them as real: the cat's just come back from an expedition somewhere like our Scruff-bag; the man just coming back from the pub after he's been and had a drink with his mates; his wife . . . she looks very young. It doesn't have to be his wife, of course. It could be his daughter. Yes, his daughter who's just written a best-selling novel about life inside a Swiss chalet. It's called, *The More You Earn, the More You Seem to Lose*. No. It's no good. They look too happy to be real.

Streaky gives Sarah her book back and then he says, 'Most of the stories were well-written but they all tended to be very similar – most of you used exactly the same plot. All except this one . . .' and he picks my book off the pile and starts to read the story out.

The brainy kids all look at each other, whispering, 'Whose is it?' and, 'Is it yours?', but none of them know. I sit and say nothing, staring at my money-box. I keep thinking that at any minute Streaky'll say how terrible it is and how he's only reading it out to show us how not to write a story, but he doesn't.

He reads it very well and uses different voices for the Customs man and for King Kong. When he gets to the part where the Customs man tells King Kong that he'll have to go into quarantine in case he's got rabies, everybody starts laughing. They laugh even more when King Kong treads on him. I even smile myself. Streaky makes it seem very funny, the way he reads it out.

When he's finished reading, Streaky says what a clever, imaginative story it is and how it would make a very good play. Everybody else in the class agrees. Then he gives the books back, or rather he stands at the front of the room and throws them. He shouts out people's names and we have to jump up and run and grab our English books as they come flying through the air, as if we're a troupe of performing sea-lions at feeding-time. When he calls my name out I just pretend I haven't heard, and my book goes skimming across the room and bounces on Sarah Swille's snout.

'Oooooh!' she squeals. I don't care. It serves her right for sitting up so straight.

'Waken your ideas up, Rebecca O'Leary,' Mr Bacon snaps.

Everybody in the class is flabbergasted when they realize that the book that Streaky's been reading the story out of is mine. They think I'm too thick to write anything more exciting than the date. I can write good stories when I feel like it, you see. And poems. It's just that I don't feel like it very often.

At dinner-time I see Bernice. I tell her about my idea of buying a present for Miss Gloucester, and she says it sounds great and she wishes she'd been the one to think of it herself. She's nice like that. She asks if she can come with me to help buy the present and choose the card. I think at first that I'd rather go on my own, but I say O.K. We agree to go to town straight after school tomorrow, just as soon as we've collected all the money from the other kids. I decide that the papers will just have to wait until later.

16

'You have seen
Sunshine and rain at once; her smiles and tears
Were like a better way . . .'

(Gentleman, Act IV, Scene III)

It just so happens that we find a card that's exactly what we want. It's very big and on the front it has a picture of a chubby pink piglet looking very drunk, standing on his hind trotters with his arms stretched out wide. Bernice draws a tiny lopsided crown on the top of his head and a bit of a black cloak coming round the edge of his shoulders and then she draws a balloon coming out of his mouth. She prints inside it: 'ALL MY KINGDOMS ARE TO BE SHARED OUT. TELL ME WHAT YOU THINK ABOUT ME!' Underneath she draws a girl's face, frowning hard and a balloon saying: 'WELL ... ER ... ER ... ERM ... I ... ER ... THINK YOU'RE JUST WONDERFUL.'

In the bottom corner of the card, where there's still some space, Bernice draws another picture. It looks great. I wish I could draw like that. She draws Gertie Runt with an arrow pointing to her shoes and a notice saying: LAUNCHING PADS. Gertie's scowling horribly and in front of her there's a picture of me, with my eyes closed and my arms outstretched, feeling at her face. 'IS THIS AN IDIOT I FEEL BEFORE ME?' it says in my balloon.

Inside the card there's a picture of some kids sitting round in a semicircle. They all look weird. One has a square head with stitches across it; one's wrapped in bandages like a mummy; another kid has ears standing up above his head like sharpened parsnips and huge bared fangs. There's a couple of cross-eyed girls sitting at the edge, one of them with a long rubbery neck that looks as if it's made out of an old inner tube, and the other one has hair that looks a bit like mine, all long and straggly. In front of them all, there's a lady just like Miss Gloucester and the balloon coming out of her mouth says: 'TODAY I WANT YOU ALL TO TRY AND IMAGINE WHAT IT FEELS LIKE TO BE A REJECT . . .'

All the kids in the Drama Group have signed their names inside the card and some of them have written their own jokes and pictures as well. It should cheer Miss Gloucester up quite a bit when she reads it.

I've bought the garden-in-a-bowl and it looks very nice. Some of the plants are rather big – especially the palm tree – and there are long snaky green and yellow striped sort of shoots dangling down around the bowl. The lads keep making jokes about it being a jungle. They call the palm tree a Triffid and keep saying how it's growing all the time when we're not looking and how it'll be taking over the whole of South Yorkshire by next week. They're daft like that. With the 80p left over we've bought a big bunch of grapes.

There are four of us going to the hospital: me and Bernice and Jonathan and Timothy Trotter. Jonathan's brought his motor bike and sidecar to take us all there. Really I can tell he's hoping that Bernice will ride on the pillion, but she's wearing high-heeled shoes and her skirt is split so far up the back that there's no way she can possibly sit on the motor bike without showing all her next week's washing to everyone we pass between our school and the Royal Hospital.

Perhaps I'd better say a quick word here about Jonathan in case you think I might be fancying him. I don't. He's tall and skinny with short blond hair and a spotty face. He's all right for a laugh but he's not really my type. I'm dying to ride on the pillion, though, because I've always wanted to ride on a motor bike and I've never had a chance before, so I start strapping on the crash helmet. Jonathan helps me, but secretly he keeps sneaking envious glances over my shoulder at Timothy Trotter who's busy trying to wedge himself into the sidecar in front of Bernice. When my helmet's fastened, Jonathan walks around to fasten down the lid of the sidecar but then Bernice screams out in agony as Timothy lurches backwards and sits on top of her. He must weigh quite a lot. I can't help laughing. We have to open up the sidecar, prise them both out and then Timothy goes in first and sits with his knees up to his chin. We can almost get Bernice in sitting in front of him, but there's no way they can hold on to the garden and the grapes as well and I can't carry them on the pillion, so they both have to be pulled out again. Then we decide to lift the seat out. Timothy sits down flat on the floor of the sidecar with his legs stretched out in front of him, clutching the grapes in his hands, and Bernice sits on top of him, holding the garden. What makes it especially funny is that Timothy's quite embarrassed because he can't think where to put his hands. Or his bunch of grapes, for that matter. Like I said before, Bernice seems to be all legs and curves, especially with her split skirt on, and Timothy has a hard job finding enough inches to hang on to without feeling as though he's going to cause her some offence. In the end he just wraps his arms around her waist like a baby gorilla, closes his eyes and hangs on.

Jonathan kicks the starter and the first thing that happens is that the sidecar lurches upwards, the grapes bounce up to the roof and the palm tree in the potted garden shoots straight up Timothy's nose. I laugh so much, I nearly fall off the bike. Then Timothy lets go of Bernice with one hand so he can poke the palm tree out of his nostril and pick up the grapes, and just then Jonathan kicks the starter again and the sidecar bounces upwards. Once more Timothy's caught completely off balance and he topples over backwards bringing Bernice down on top of him. Jonathan and me are just about hysterical. All you can see in the sidecar are arms, legs, flying grapes and an extremely interesting view up Bernice Berkshire's split skirt.

And we're off. Jonathan wheels the motor bike down on to the road and, as we set off round the corner, I remember about how the person on the pillion has to lean over to balance it and I lean over so enthusiastically in the wrong direction that the sidecar nearly takes off.

At first I'm terrified. I seem to get jolted in the air every time we go over a little stone in the road and I nearly have a heart attack when we get sandwiched in between two double-decker buses, but after that it's great. You feel as though you're going at a fantastic high speed when you're on the back of a motor bike although really I don't suppose we are going all that fast. You have to remember to hold on very tightly when you go round corners and you don't feel very safe at first but, apart from that, it's fantastic. The only other snag about it is that it's cold.

When we arrive at the hospital my hands are just about numb with cold. My legs aren't too warm either. They're so stiff that I have a real job levering myself off the pillion and then I march around like a Frankenstein monster trying to bring back feeling to my legs and toes. My fingers just feel like swollen lumps of raspberry jelly and it's ages before I can get the helmet undone.

When we come to open the sidecar, the perspex top is so steamed up that you can't see anything inside. I don't know what's been happening in there, but it must have involved an awful lot of heavy breathing. We open up the top, prise out Timothy and Bernice and spend the next five minutes trying to get our circulation going again. We pick up some of the grapes from the floor of the sidecar and put them back in the bag and try to straighten out the worst of the creases in the palm tree. Then we set off to find the right ward.

Miss Gloucester's ward is on the next-to-top floor so

Jonathan (who likes to think he's in charge of this expedition) suggests we take the lift. It's one of those old-fashioned iron ones like a pit shaft with great big clanging doors that make you feel as if you're travelling in a high-altitude gibbon cage. We pile in and press the button. Nothing happens. Then we shut the inside gate. It clangs like a prison cage in a horror film and we can hear the sound echoing round the empty corridors. Still the lift won't work, so we open the inside gate, reach through and clang the outside gate closed, fasten the inside gate again and, before we've time to press the button once more, the lift lurches upwards and nearly sends us flying.

It jerks upwards very slowly. Painfully slowly. It would have been much quicker to walk up all the stairs. As we stare out through the bars, we can see the numbers of the different floors as we float past them . . . 2 . . . 3 . . . 4. . . . We want floor five. It comes to five and we grab hold of the cage handle ready to leap out when it stops. But the lift goes sailing past, leaving us gaping down like idiots at the big notice saying Floor 5 sinking out of sight.

'Oh yeah,' sneers Timothy, trying to do an imitation of Jonathan's voice. *'Let's take the lift – it'll be a lot faster*. We could have walked there and back by now.'

'Some of us could,' says Jonathan, pretending to be scornful. 'Some of us that are fit . . .'

'And slim . . .' adds Bernice.

'I was only thinking about you puffing up all those stairs, Trotter.'

Fortunately, floor six is the top. There's nobody waiting when we arrive, so we all press the button again for floor five – about six times each – and then the lift starts staggering down again. We look down and see floor five looming up towards us and, of course, the lift goes floating straight past again without so much as slowing down.

'Oh no,' we all groan together.

'We'll have to get out and walk up,' says Bernice.

We see floor four coming closer and the lift doesn't seem to be slowing down so we all start panicking. Like an idiot, I do something completely ridiculous. I see a red button on its own at the side of the lift and I press it. It has a little notice next to it that says EMERGENCY.

'Idiot!' screeches Jonathan, as the lift skids to a halt half-way between floors four and five.

'Well, it's an emergency, isn't it?' I moan at him.

'No,' sighs Timothy in disgust. 'It isn't. We won't half get into trouble. We'd better get out before anybody comes.'

We look down in horror at the fourth floor, about four and a half feet below us, but Bernice has already started opening the gates. She plonks the garden-in-a-bowl on top of Timothy's grapes and sits on the edge of the lift. When she sees the height of the drop, she changes her mind and turns round to lower herself down with her arms, like Jane swinging down to meet Tarzan. The lads keep making stupid comments like: 'Look out, there's a gibbon about,' and 'Shall we tickle her?', and then Jonathan starts making idiotic Tarzan noises. Bernice is still dangling and trying to find the best way to jump when this old-aged pensioner comes doddering up the stairs. When he sees Bernice he stops and glares and looks as if he's going to have a heart attack. Not only is he amazed at seeing this girl swinging from the lift shaft like an escaped trapeze artiste, but the view he's getting up her split skirt looks as if it could be definitely dangerous for his health. I can understand now why Bernice was so keen to go down first.

She jumps and lands safely. I'm laughing so much I can hardly get out of the lift, but in the end, I do. Then we have quite a few little problems with Timothy Trotter and the garden and the grapes, and we finish up having to spend another five minutes straightening out the extra creases in the palm tree, unravelling bits of striped creeper from Timothy's earhole and chasing some more of the grapes across the floor of the landing. There are still plenty of grapes left, but by now most of them are loose in the bottom of the brown paper bag and looking a bit the worse for wear.

We have several attempts at closing the lift gates but there's no way it can be done. In the end, we have to set off and leave them. We're late already. As we dash around the corner we nearly collide with a nurse pushing a man in a wheelchair over towards the lift. I don't know how she's going to wheel him up that four-and-a-half-foot gap. I think about going after her and offering to help but I decide against it. We've wasted enough time already.

17

'Where is thy lustre now?'

(Cornwall, Act III, Scene VII)

I'm surprised how ill Miss Gloucester looks. She's sitting in bed, propped up with white pillows and wearing a plain white nightdress. Her hair is brushed back from her face and held in place by a plain elasticated band. She looks very pale and tired. I've never noticed her looking like that at school. It's amazing how much worse people always look when they get inside a hospital.

'Hello,' we say, grinning and trying to get our breath back. 'How are you?'

'Hello. Not so bad.' She smiles and eases herself higher on the pillows.

'We've brought you a present,' says Bernice, holding out the garden very cleverly so that the creased-up palm tree is at the side furthest away from Miss Gloucester.

'Oh! That's lovely.' She looks really pleased and reaches out her hands to take the bowl. 'That's very kind of you.'

Bernice ignores the outstretched hands and carefully puts the garden down on the bedside locker, still with the creased-up palm tree at the back. Then she stands in front of it.

Miss Gloucester won't be put off. 'Oh, let me see it properly,' she says. 'It looks gorgeous. Did I really see a palm tree at the back there?' She reaches out her hands again. 'I've always wanted a palm tree.'

Bernice finally gives up trying to conceal the damage. She stands aside and then passes the bowl to Miss Gloucester. 'We had a bit of trouble with the lift,' she says apologetically, trying to squash down the striped creeper into its proper place.

'Not to mention the motor bike,' adds Timothy Trotter with a wistful look at Bernice.

'Oh dear. What a shame!' Miss Gloucester says as she tries to uncrumple the palm tree. 'I'm sure it'll straighten itself out when it's been watered, though. I don't think that you've spoiled it.'

'We've bought you some grapes as well.' Timothy grins as if this is going to compensate for the squashed garden. He holds the paper bag up and pulls out an enormous grape branch that's completely bare apart from two miserable little grapes still dangling on the end of its stalk. 'They're just sort of . . . sort of . . . *loose*.'

'Thank you . . . very much.' Miss Gloucester smiles and tries hard to look as if they're the nicest presents anybody's ever bought for her.

Actually, when you look around, it seems quite possible that they might be. Everybody else's lockers are piled up high with cards and flowers and bowls of fruit, but Miss Gloucester's is almost empty. She has only one card. It's strange that. I've never thought of her having nobody to come and visit her in hospital. You don't think of teachers as being without friends.

Miss Gloucester inspects the grapes and passes them round and everybody takes one even though we all know where they've been and realize that it isn't terribly hygienic to eat them. Then I take the card out of my pocket. I show it to Miss Gloucester and she laughs at all the jokes and silly pictures and looks a lot more cheerful. I thought she would. When she's finished reading the card, I stand it on the locker and glance at the other one. It's from Gertie Runt.

'Has Gertie . . . I mean . . . has Miss Runt been to see

you?' I ask her. I didn't know they were even on speaking terms.

'Yes,' says Miss Gloucester with her mouth full of grapes. 'I thought it was very nice of her. She brought me a card and some talcum powder.'

That makes me feel really sorry for her. If Gertie Runt is Miss Gloucester's only friend, then I'd hate to think what her enemies would be like. 'Very nice,' I mumble.

'Yes, and she's been so busy as well,' Miss Gloucester goes on, helping herself to another grape whilst there's still a few left. 'She says that she's organizing a trip to France. Are any of you going?'

The others look at each other – just for a tiny fraction of a second – but long enough for me to realize that this is something they don't want to talk about in front of me. Bernice hesitates and then opens her mouth. 'Yes,' she says. 'Us three are going – me and Jonathan and Tim.'

I start to take a sudden extra interest in Gertie Runt's card on the locker top. I don't know where to put myself. 'Didn't you want to go, Rebecca?' Miss Gloucester asks me.

I open my mouth to say I'd hate it, but change my mind. 'I couldn't afford it,' I tell her. 'Dad's been off work a lot this year.'

'Oh dear,' she says. 'I didn't know . . .'

Just then this enormous nurse rolls up. She looms over us like a tower of granite. 'Patients are only allowed two visitors,' she bellows. 'Two of you will have to go.'

'Oh, I'm sorry,' Bernice says straightaway. She always likes to keep on the right side of people. 'We'll go and chat to some people who haven't got any visitors,' she offers, and breezes off down the ward, smiling like Miss World at a charity ball.

Now I think I've mentioned before that Bernice is very attractive. She's the sort of girl that has this hypnotic sort of effect on lads. They follow her everywhere. And that's just what happens. She prances off down the ward like Lady Muck and the two lads just turn around and follow her. Like page boys.

I smile. Don't think I'm jealous. I just think it's very funny.

'Rebecca,' Miss Gloucester says, looking a bit embarrassed, 'I've just been thinking. I hope you won't be offended if I . . .'

Oh no. What's she going to say now? That lads'd follow me like that if I didn't have such bad breath? Or B.O.? I make up my mind that I'll try not to be offended and I walk over to her side of the bed. 'No,' I say. 'What is it?'

'I wanted to suggest something . . . about the trip to France. Look,' she swallows hard and looks directly at me for the first time, 'we always have money available in school for people who can't afford to go on trips. In fact, we decided to use some of the money from the last school drama production . . . it's not easy to know who to ask, you see . . .'

'No,' I say and smile at her. She's more embarrassed about this than I am.

'In fact, Miss Runt only mentioned it the other day when she came,' Miss Gloucester goes on. 'Miss Hoggit has asked her if there was anyone we could pay for to go on the trip and she couldn't think of anybody.' She leans over and looks at me in a pleading sort of way. 'Really, Rebecca, they would love to be able to use the money . . . if you think you'd like to go . . .'

'I don't know.' To tell you the truth, the idea of spending three whole weeks in France with Gertie Runt isn't really all that exciting.

'I know it must have been difficult at home for you these last twelve months,' Miss Gloucester insists, 'and I think it would be good for you to get away with people of your own age. I think you'd enjoy it.'

I think about what a good laugh the four of us have had

coming here tonight and realize that perhaps she might be right. 'Yes,' I say. 'I think I might.'

'Would you mind mentioning it to Miss Hoggit?' Miss Gloucester asks kindly. 'I suppose I could write . . . but I think she'd appreciate it if you went and asked her yourself.'

Oh yes, I can just imagine it. I haven't even seen Miss Hoggit since I screamed and swore at her. Asking her to cough up a hundred and fifty pounds to send me to France would go down really fantastic. I can't think of anything to say.

'Will you ask her then?'

I'll have to try and find a way round it somehow. 'O.K.,' I mutter.

Just then, the nurse comes back to tell all the visitors it's time to go home. The other three walk across to say good-night and Miss Gloucester looks quite sad that we're going. We haven't really been here all that long. She thanks us several times again for the presents, which seems a bit unnecessary as the garden doesn't really look all that exciting now and all that's left of the bunch of grapes is an empty stalk and a dirty brown paper bag. 'Look,' she says, when we're just getting ready to go, 'I really am sorry about the play. You all worked so hard. I feel very bad about having to leave it all in the middle . . .'

'Oh no,' Bernice interrupts. 'We've all really enjoyed the rehearsals, haven't we?'

She looks around and we all nod and agree with her. 'It doesn't matter about putting on the play – honestly, it doesn't,' she insists. Like I say, Bernice is always the first one to say the right thing to people.

'The practices were great,' says Tim. 'We had a good laugh.'

'I enjoyed them very much,' I add.

Miss Gloucester smiles and looks pleased. 'Anyway,' she says, 'it looks as though you'll have to finish the play off on your own.' She pauses. 'You'll have to think up your own endings . . .'

I don't know what she means by that. The big bulldozer of a nurse comes back to shovel us out of the ward so we have to say good-bye. But I keep wondering what Miss Gloucester means. How could we finish the play off without her? What does she mean by thinking up our own endings? I really don't know what to make of it.

18

'Blow, winds, and crack your cheeks! rage! blow!
You cataracts and hurricanoes . . .'

(Lear, Act III, Scene II)

There's going to be a storm. I hear it thundering when I set off to deliver the rest of the papers and at first I don't mind because it's that nervous, tensed-up darkened sky that I like so much. Quivering with electricity and as still as a graveyard. Then it starts to rain – a great big cloudburst of stinging raindrops and I have to try and squeeze myself flat against somebody's front door to try and keep my face from getting washed off. I dread the people looking out of the window and seeing me but I can't squeeze myself flat enough to keep out of sight. I'm not exactly streamlined. Then the papers start to get soggy, so I have to go on even though the rain's still pouring down.

Before long, my socks are squelching and the rain is streaming down from the tip of my nose like a water chute. Nobody else is out. The lightning flashes in the sky like a special effect from a Dracula film and the thunder growls and rumbles at me, and then crashes in my earhole so suddenly it makes me jump. I start to feel scared. Like I say, I'm the only person in the world who's out doing a paper round tonight. Everybody else is somewhere sensible – like hiding under the table. There's an enormous flash of lightning just as I'm posting a paper through a letter-box and I jump backwards in horror. I wonder if I could be electrocuted from touching the metal letter-box and a soggy newspaper at the same time, but there's nobody about to ask. There never is when you need them.

*

When I arrive home I am, of course, soaking wet. My mum always told me that you should never sit around steaming in wet clothes when you've been out in the rain, so I decide to have a bath and go to bed early. I make myself a mug of hot milk to take to bed as well. You see, you have to learn to look after yourself when there's nobody else to bother. When I've had my drink, I decide to read for a while before I go to sleep. After a bit I hear the back door open. My father's come home.

I listen to him stumbling about downstairs and try to work out whether he's just a little bit drunk, or average, or whether he's tanked up to the eyebrows. He sounds pretty far gone tonight I think. I hear him staggering through the hall and into the front room and I imagine him collapsed on one of the armchairs by the fire, soggy and bloated like a capsized Walrus.

I try to forget about him and settle down to sleep instead when, suddenly, I remember about my paper money. I've left it in my purse downstairs in the hall. What if he pinches it? He must be broke still or else he'd have put something back in my money-box by now and I don't see why I should nearly catch my death of pneumonia, tramping round the streets all night in raging thunderstorms, just to keep him in beer money.

I can just imagine him starting to stagger through the hall and up to bed, stumbling and pulling himself upright with the shelf, nearly knocking the plant pots flying and then catching sight of my Bunny purse and opening the little zip between its ears . . . looking inside . . . counting out the pound notes . . .

I climb out of bed, wedge my feet inside my slippers and put my dressing-gown on. Then I slowly start to tiptoe down the stairs. It takes me a long time. I walk downstairs very carefully, trying not to make a noise, because I don't want him to hear me. I don't want him to ask me why I'm out of bed. I don't want to lie to him. I hate telling lies.

And, whilst I'm creeping down the stairs, I strain my ears to listen for noises from the living-room – noises that might tell me what he's doing. And I can hear the silence in the hallway, and outside I can hear the pattering of rain and the distant rolls of thunder. I can hear another sound as well that at first I don't recognize. I walk further down the stairs. The sound is coming from the living-room; it's a kind of low and stilted, howling noise. Like a wolf. A grey wolf choking with its throat stuffed tight with cotton wool. I can't understand it. I stop and listen for a moment and then I move slowly forward again into the hallway. Listening. And the noise comes again – a kind of choked howling noise and it sounds strange and unearthly; like an omen of despair.

I walk past the shelf where my purse is. I don't feel for it or switch the light on, but keep on moving forwards like someone in a trance. I have to find out what's happening.

I stand outside the door of the living-room and peer through the crack at the side, but I can't see anything. I start breathing in very shallow little gasps so that I don't make any noise. I can hear the sounds more clearly now. They don't really sound like an animal but they don't sound human either; they sound ghostly and pale, like a dead spirit wailing. And in between the wails come little stifled gasps and sobs. I know what it is, though. It's my father. And he's crying.

19

'The oldest hath borne most: we that are young
Shall never see so much, nor live so long.'

(Edgar, Act V, Scene III)

Slowly, I reach for the door handle and then I move the door steadily forward. Quietly. I want to see what's happening. I know my father's sitting in there and I know my father's crying, but I have to look at him. I have to see him. I move closer and put my eye to the opening in the doorway but still the space is narrow. I can only see the windowsill and the edge of the table. I can't see any movement in the room. I ease the door forward a bit more. Stealthily. Still hardly daring to breathe. And the sounds are changing now. Little gasps and sobs. They're starting to sound less ghostly and animal-like and more like a person. More like a person crying.

I have to know what's happening. Very quietly, I ease the door open several inches wide. It moves so silently that you might think it was just being blown by the breeze. I can see inside now. I can see as far as the armchair by the fireplace and I can see him sitting there. He's leaning forward with his head down on his hands and I can see his shoulders shaking. Shaking with the sobs. His whole body is shaking as though it's racked with pain. I don't know what to do. I feel afraid.

I move my head away from the doorway in case he should look up, but still I can't go back upstairs. I try putting my eye to the crack on the other side, but it's no good. I can see a thin sliver of light and nothing else. I feel very strange. I feel as though I have to be here but still I know I'm trespassing. I have to see him, though. I move back to the other side of the door and ease it forward just another inch or two – ever so gently – and now my face will fit inside the gap – and half my shoulder – and I can see him properly. Sitting there.

He doesn't hear me and he doesn't look up. He still has his head down buried in his hands and he looks pathetic. He's wearing these skin-tight jeans and I can see the fat of his stomach bulging out over the top beneath his shirt. His shirt is new and expensive and made of white denim, only now it's got a big brown stain right down the middle. It looks like beer. The shirt is open nearly down to his waist and his hairy chest is covered with Nosun which is supposed to make him look suntanned. We never go on holiday. He wears a crucifix – a long, silver one and his hair is black and curled down into his neck. Usually it's styled and blow-waved when he's going out but tonight it looks a mess. All of him looks a mess. He looks so old. He looks so ancient and yet he's wearing all these flash clothes like a teenager. He never did that when Mum was here. He's got no right to look like that. He looks pathetic.

I don't know what to do. I stand in the doorway, terrified still, and stare at him. He starts moaning again, crying out loud like a baby with great big sobs pulsing through his body. I stand transfixed, glaring at him. Then, very slowly, painfully, I see him lift his head up from his hands and stare at the half-empty glass standing on the other side of the table beside him. And when I see his face I feel shivers of horror pass through me like shuddering ghosts. His face is bright red and swollen round the cheeks and eyelids. It looks deformed. His eyes are bulging and bloodshot, and tears are streaming down his face. I don't think he could see me even if he turned his face and looked. I don't think he can even see the glass in front of him. But I don't want to risk it. I have to move away out of sight.

Then, just before I move, I feel a sense of something

very strange. It's not easy to explain what goes through my head – in fact, really it never gets inside my head; it's more of an emotion. A feeling. Something touches me, deep and fiercely like a needle prodding at a nerve. Something I can't understand. Something touches me and I feel afraid. What happens is that just for a tiny, minute fraction of a second, I feel this urge to go inside the room and run across to my father and . . . this sounds incredible . . . I want to kneel down in front of him and put my arms around his neck. I want to comfort him.

I don't do it, of course. I stand there, waiting, staring at him and ignore the needle poking at me. The yearning in my head. And I let the scene soak slowly inside my brain and become a part of me.

I leave the door ajar as I creep back up the stairs and I feel a terrifying emptiness swirling like a mist around me. I lay my head on my pillow and try to think about nothing, but the picture's still there. Engraved inside my skull. I think it will lie there for ever.

On Sunday I go to the Meeting House again. I arrive early and go straight into the room where they have the Meeting because I don't want anybody to come across and talk to me. I want to be by myself.

The room smells of musty old wood and I can hear the Cathedral bells ringing outside as I walk right across to the far side of the long bench seat and sit down in the corner. I close my eyes and try to think of nothing.

There's something wrong with my mind today. I don't know what it is, but I can't concentrate on anything. When you come to a Meeting you're supposed to meditate, and that means thinking about things that are really important or emptying your head so that the Silence can seep in; but today my mind just flits around from one thought to another and none of them are important. I look around and fidget.

As it gets near to half-past ten, the Meeting House fills up. People come and sit along the benches. When anyone heads in my direction, I glare at them and they change their minds and sit somewhere else. Before very long, though, the seats are filling up so people are forced to come and sit near me. I stare down at my feet and try to ignore them. A man comes in late and I have to move up a few inches for him to squeeze in next to me. I wish it wouldn't get so crowded; you can't think straight with all these people near you.

Like I say, I don't seem able to concentrate today. I look at the backs of people's heads and wonder what they're all thinking about and then I run my fingers up and down the seams of my jeans and cross my legs and uncross them. A woman reads from the *Advices and Queries* – we've got that book at home because my mother used to read it. 'Live simply,' the woman says and talks about it but I don't take any notice because you can't live much more simply than I do. I think about what we're going to have for dinner.

Later on, a woman at the other side of the room stands up and talks about her father dying. I wasn't feeling too cheerful when I came in here this morning and I don't think this will help. She talks about how well she gets on with her mother, who is still alive, but how she never really liked her father. Well, that's not unusual.

I stare hard at the shadows on the ceiling and try not to listen. She talks about something called mis-spent opportunities and how there's a right time for doing everything and if you let the right time pass, you spend the rest of your life regretting it and feeling guilty. She starts to say how we always know when the time is right because we get these promptings from God. I think about the other night when I saw my father crying and the way I wanted to run across and comfort him, but then I shut my mind off. You can only listen to so much. I run my hand along the smooth worn wood at the edge of the bench and try to count the number of people in the Meeting who've got beards. But you can't always tell from the back. Then I count those who're bald.

This woman's still talking. As I say, I don't want to listen. It reminds me too much of things I don't want to think about but then, all of a sudden, there's a coincidence. Something that makes me open my ears and start to pay attention. She talks about *King Lear*. She doesn't talk about the part of the play that we've been doing in Drama, but the end of the play that I don't know anything about yet. It seems as though Cordelia, the daughter King Lear was horrible to, has come back to meet him at Dover and they both want to be nice to each other. But now King Lear's grown mad and he doesn't even recognize her and then, when he does, it's too late because she's dead. The woman reads this verse out from the end of the play, reciting it slowly so that each word seeps inside my brain like dirty washing left to soak:

> 'The weight of this sad time we must obey;
> Speak what we feel, not what we ought to say.
> The oldest hath borne most: we that are young
> Shall never see so much nor live so long.'

She pauses. The needles are out again, red hot, twisting into my nerves, touching me. The woman talks about how much she wanted to talk to her father before he died. How she wished she had the courage to explain her feelings to him. 'Speak what we feel,' she says again.

And I think of my father crying. Waiting for someone to come in through the door and put their arms around him. Waiting for someone to comfort him. Waiting for me.

And it's just as if fingers of tempered steel are probing inside me, searching for raw wires. An exposed nerve end. And, suddenly, the contact's made. The pain and tension and the restlessness come swelling and bubbling from inside me and a great sob retches out of my body like a drowning person coming up for air. My lip starts trembling as if the bottom half of my face has come loose and it's completely out of control, waving about and making me feel like a complete idiot.

'The weight of this sad time we must obey,' she goes on, as if I haven't heard her right the first time, and she starts talking again about obeying the promptings of God inside us. And these great sobs rise up inside my throat and escape from me – here, with all these people – when everything's so quiet – and I try to pretend I've just got hiccups or a bad cough or something but I can't. I just have to sob. Loudly and openly.

'The oldest hath borne most,' she says. And then the tears well up inside my eyes and overflow and come streaming down my cheeks like melted hailstones. I'm crying now, my whole body shaking with sobs, and my nose keeps running. I sniff and try to wipe away the tears, but they just keep streaming downwards like a flood.

Nobody looks at me. There's no way they can't hear me because I'm making so much noise you could hear it outside in the street but nobody wants to make me feel embarrassed. The woman keeps on talking through all the sniffs and sobs and little whimpers that keep escaping from me. 'The oldest hath borne most,' she says once more and I see my father crying again and I know what she means. Suddenly, *I know* . . .

I rub my eyes and see nothing but a swollen mist. I sniff hard and then someone pushes a handkerchief into my hand. The person next to me has moved up closer and I take the hankie thankfully and blow my nose, loudly, and start to wipe the tears. Then a strange thing happens. I feel someone touch my arm. This man who was sitting next to me has moved up and now he's gripping my arm with his hand as if to steady me. The sobs begin to ease a little and then he takes my hand and pats it. Slowly and rhythmically. Gently.

He's not afraid of coming up to me, this stranger, and comforting me. He's not afraid to touch me. He's not afraid to take my wrist and hold it firm. And pat my hand.

This stranger who doesn't know me at all; this man who's never even seen me before can comfort me like a friend.

And I can't comfort anyone.

20

'Striving to better, oft we mar what's well.'

(Albany, Act 1, Scene IV)

When I get home, I walk upstairs to my bedroom, and, when I open the door, my father's standing there with my money-box in his hand.

We stare at each other. I don't know what to say. I think about what happened at the Meeting House and I try not to be angry. I wait for him to say something.

He looks away from me as if he's embarrassed. 'I'm sorry,' he says. 'I came to put the money back.'

I don't say anything. I still can't think what to say.

'You weren't needing it, were you?' he asks me. 'You didn't miss it . . . did you?'

I open my mouth to snarl at him but I don't. I think about him crying. 'I was going to have my hair done,' I tell him. 'I was saving up to have it permed.' I don't actually smile at him or anything but I try not to sound too horrible.

'Oh,' he says, and there's another pause. 'Well, you can still have it done,' he goes on. 'I've put the money back now. I only borrowed it for a few days. I didn't think you'd miss it.'

There's another silence whilst I try to decide how much I want to tell him. I couldn't start to explain about Darren, that's for sure. 'It's too late now,' I say at last. 'I was going to have it done for when I went to the disco at the youth club but that was last week-end.'

'I'm sorry.'

*

Downstairs, I get dinner ready. I put a cup of tea down on the table for him to drink whilst I'm dishing the baked beans out, but when he comes into the kitchen he just ignores it and takes a can of beer out of the fridge instead.

By the time we start our dinner, he's half-way through the second can. I suck my cheeks in and tap my fingers on the table. I cut away some of the burnt crust off my toast and then pause and glance up at him. 'You drink too much,' I say.

He looks at me over the top of his glass and his face seems hurt again and sad. I'm very surprised at what he answers. 'Do you think I haven't noticed?' he says.

There doesn't seem an easy answer to that. You see, I'd always thought of drinking as something he did on purpose – out of spite even. I've never thought of him not wanting to drink or trying to stop. It makes it seem different when he talks about it like that. 'You never used to drink,' I go on. 'Not as much . . . not when Mum was here.'

He thinks about this for a minute or two as he munches his way through a mouthful of baked beans. I don't know why, but we've never talked about this before. It didn't seem right to mention it somehow. Not before today.

He swallows hard and pauses before he picks up another forkful of toast. 'Your mother never used to like me to drink,' he says, as though that explains it all. I suppose he thinks I thrive on watching him booze himself into a stupor.

I suck my cheeks in, harder. 'Do you think *I* like it then?' I ask him.

He looks a bit shocked, embarrassed even. 'Why?' he asks me. 'Do you mind?'

Do I mind? Sitting up at night and listening to him retching in the garden? Seeing him lying in bed as if he's in a coma when he should be going to work? How could anybody not mind? What does he think I am?

I sigh and glare at him. 'Yes,' I tell him. 'Yes, I do mind.'

He looks surprised that I seem to care so much. 'Oh,' he says, sort of taken aback and carries on with his dinner.

After a couple of minutes, he pushes the burnt crusts of his toast to one side and rests his knife and fork down in the centre of his plate. 'I really am sorry about the money,' he says again, shaking his head slowly and staring down at the floor. 'I never thought you'd be saving up for anything special.'

'It's O.K.,' I tell him again. What else is there to say?

'Listen,' he goes on, 'why don't you have it done this Saturday? We could go out together then . . . the two of us – go out for a meal or something.'

I try not to let him see me shudder. Go out with my father? It seems ridiculous. What if somebody saw us out together in the street? I'd never live it down.

I cut a corner off my toast and pile some squashed baked beans on to it. They're all modged up together from when they got burnt at the bottom of the pan. I haven't had a decent meal for ages. Perhaps the restaurant wouldn't be such a bad idea after all. I swallow hard and take a deep breath.

'O.K.,' I say. 'I'll do that.'

I feel a right idiot, sitting in this posh hairdresser's with my hair all shampooed and wet, waiting to have a re-style. I've never had a hair-do before. My mum always used to trim my hair herself and I haven't had it cut since she died. I've just worn it long and straight. There's all these posh women sitting around with ludicrous hair-styles that look like plastic birds' nests. I'd hate to have my hair done like that. There's one woman in front of me with a thing like a swimming cap on her head. It's covered in holes and bits of her hair are sticking out of them like a hedgehog. She looks ridiculous. Then this little hair-dresser called Nigel gets a sort of paintbrush and he starts painting her hair with it. I realize now what's happening: she's having blond streaks painted on her hair.

Another woman's had her hair dyed purple. They're all sitting round with stacks of make-up on and jewellery and cigarettes in long holders. Talking about the price of dog food and what happened last night on some serial for morons on the television.

Whilst I'm waiting for my turn, this assistant comes and brings me a cup of coffee and a pile of magazines. He's a boy that left our school last year. He's wearing a little badge on his shirt that says MR E.G. BERTILLE on it. That's stupid. We used to call him Egbert at school. He pretends he doesn't know me and just leaves me the coffee and the magazines and hobbles away in his high-heeled cowboy boots.

I sip the coffee, which is much too weak and milky, and I turn over the pages of one of the magazines. It's mostly advertisements for stupid things that nobody needs, like plastic finger-nails and powder puffs, but then I start reading an article about this fantastic new rock group that's in the charts this week. They're really good. There's a full-page photograph of their lead singer and suddenly I realize that that's how I want my hair done. Just like her. On the top it's very short and bristly, rather like a scrubbing brush, with different coloured streaks – but not like the woman in the swimming cap. I suddenly realize that I've always wanted my hair done like that, ever since I can remember. The style probably only came out this year, but it doesn't matter. That's still how I've always wanted my hair to look.

Another hairdresser comes over and puts this sort of pinny on me, back to front, and I notice that his hair has blond streaks in it as well. I take the magazine with me to the cutting chair and, when I show him the photograph, his eyebrows shoot upwards as if I've just shown him a photo of somebody in the nude. He looks quite shocked.

He smiles at first as if he thinks I'm joking but then, when I've told him I'm serious, he sits me down and combs my hair, lifting it off my face and contemplating my reflection in the mirror. 'Mmmmmmmm . . .' he says, still looking thoughtfully at me. 'Mmmmmmmm . . .' He pushes my head around so that he can look at my face from different angles. It's as if he's judging a lopsided cabbage at a gardening show. He keeps frowning and looking first at the photograph and then back at my reflection in the mirror. 'Mmmmmmm . . .' he mutters again, and then he looks back at the photograph once more. 'Yes,' he says finally, reaching for the scissors. 'Yes, I think it might suit you.'

21

'I am a man
More sinn'd against than sinning.'
(Lear, Act III, Scene II)

I feel really excited about my hair. It looks fantastic. I walk out of the hairdresser's into the busy streets and, although it's nearly tea-time now, it's still a gorgeous day. The sun is shining, very low down in the sky and casting long dramatic shadows. The leaves are just coming out on the trees that line the main road, so there's this pale, lime-coloured sort of green lit up by the sun settling down behind it and it looks gorgeous. Really beautiful.

I see some lads from school on the other side of the road. I think first of all about walking past and ignoring them, but I don't. I smile and wave. They stare back at me as if I'm a Martian that's just landed from outer space. I'm not bothered. I can't wait for my dad to see my hair.

I nearly trip up over Scruffbag as I go running down the path to the back door. He's been gone so long this time, I was beginning to think he must have emigrated.

He follows me as I walk into the kitchen and shut the door. Then he gets a proper look at me for the first time. He arches his back and bares his teeth as he reverses into the corner. 'It's only me, Scruffbag,' I say, trying to sound reassuring, but he continues to look at me with the same expression on his face as he had when next-door's Alsatian bit his tail.

The door of the kitchen opens and Dad walks in with a big smile on his face. 'Hel . . . lo,' he says. The smile changes as swiftly as if he's just said good evening to a Gorgon.

'Hello. Do you like it?'

He stares hard at me and then walks round me in a circle ... very slowly ... as if he's inspecting a grounded flying saucer. I try to read something from his face but it's completely expressionless. I think he must be suffering from shock.

'Well, it's ...' He searches for a suitable adjective, but it doesn't come easily. 'It's ... it's ... unusual,' he says at last, as if there's no other word to describe it.

'I know, but do you like it?'

'Mmmmmm ...' He doesn't sound ever so sure about it. 'Mmmmmm ... well ... well ... well, it's different ... isn't it? It makes a change.'

To be honest, he doesn't sound terribly enthusiastic, but I'm not bothered. I hang my jacket up and then dash upstairs to have a bath and get changed for going out. I keep looking at myself in the mirror whilst I'm waiting for the bath to fill up. It's great when you can't remember what you look like and you have to keep reminding yourself.

I drag out the only pair of jeans that are washed and ironed and I put them on and change my shirt. I even put a bit of make-up on – just to make it look as if I think it's an occasion. When I go downstairs, he's waiting in the hall, looking at himself in the mirror. That's just typical. He's wearing very tight black cord jeans, a white open-necked shirt and his black zip-up jacket. I start to feel worried again in case I see anybody I know whilst we're out. I wish we'd got a car so I didn't have to walk down the road with him.

'Are you ready?' He turns around and looks at me, and you can tell by the shocked expression on his face that he hasn't got used to my hairstyle yet.

'Yeah. Come on.'

We walk out of the front door and set off down the road.

*

Everything's O.K. until we get down to the High Street. It's early evening now, so the Chinese chip shop and the off-licence are both open and there are lots of kids hanging about together in the street. As we reach the crossing opposite the chip shop, I see quite a few kids from school that I recognize – mostly older ones – some of them from the Drama Group. I notice Bernice first of all (she's the sort of girl you'd notice on Blackpool beach on August Bank Holiday Monday), and then I notice Jonathan and some others in the fifth year. I decide it might be best to let my father walk on a few steps in front, so I pause and bend down to adjust one of the laces on my trainers. I don't know whether I ought to wave to Bernice or not.

Then something amazing happens. The next few seconds are sort of slowed down in my mind because in a way they're so incredible. If you were just walking past, though, you wouldn't see anything at all. It's just something very small that makes an enormous difference to me. What happens is this: whilst I'm bending down and messing with my shoe-lace, I glance across at the other side of the road to see whether the kids there have noticed me or not, and they haven't. Bernice Berkshire is looking ... no, staring ... across the road towards the crossing where my father's standing, waiting for the traffic to stop. She's staring at him, open-mouthed. Then she taps the girl next to her on the shoulder and points, and the other girl starts ogling too. Both of them stand there, staring at my father, as if he's the most incredible piece of talent in the High Street. It's amazing. What's even more fantastic is that, when I look up at him myself – and he's quite a few yards away by this time, remember – I can actually see what they're getting at. Provided that you look at him from quite a long way off, my father is incredibly handsome.

He's tall, so you don't notice how fat he is until you get

close up; he walks very straight and upright (considering how old he is!) and he wears his leather jacket with the big collar turned upwards and his hands inside the sideways pockets at the front. The black jacket shows off how white his shirt is and his artificial suntan is actually very effective when you're looking at him from the other side of the road. I'm looking at him, you see, in a completely different light from how I usually do. I'm looking at my father through Bernice Berkshire's eyes and it's quite uncanny.

As the traffic stops, he turns around to see where I've got to and by this time I've come running up behind him. He puts his arm around my shoulders, protectively, to steer me across the road and I feel a touch of something I would never have imagined possible. I feel a touch of pride. As we reach the other side of the road and turn down to go to Marco's Restaurant, I just glance up and see the kids all staring. I think they're wondering who I am. I give a little wave and a bit of a smile but they don't look any wiser. They'll realize when I get to school on Monday.

We spend five minutes looking at the menu and decide we can't cope with the spaghetti. It used to be my favourite but I seem to have gone off it a bit just lately. I decide to risk lasagne instead. Dad orders a pizza and a small bottle of wine for us to share.

Whilst we're waiting for the meal to be cooked, he suddenly says to me, 'I like your hair, you know. I'm glad you had it done.'

'Oh.' That's surprising. 'I thought you weren't really all that keen.'

'Well, it's different, isn't it?' he says. 'It's your own personality . . . sort of . . . coming through . . .'

The wine arrives and he pours us both a glass. It doesn't taste too bad. I don't know what he means about my personality. 'How do you mean?' I ask him. Because if my personality's only just started coming through, I don't know who I've been living with for the past fourteen years.

He pauses for quite a long time, staring into his wine glass. 'Your mother was a very strong character,' he says at last. 'She had a very forceful personality.'

My mind races backwards and forwards over this, struggling to find the link between my new hairstyle and my mother. It doesn't come.

'Some of her ideas were very strong . . . things she approved of or disapproved of, you know?' He glances up at me to see what sort of reaction this is getting.

I'm not really sure what to think. I can't bear anybody to criticize my mother. 'She was a fantastic person,' I tell him.

'Yes. Yes, of course she was,' he answers. 'That's why . . . that's why she still has this amazing influence over us both. Even now . . .' he concentrates hard to find the exact words he wants to say . . . 'even now, I can imagine her standing behind me and scowling if I buy clothes I don't really need or . . . like this . . .' he points to the bottle of wine standing on the table between us. 'I feel guilty, doing anything she wouldn't have approved of. Sometimes I think I'll always feel like that. It's not easy to get away from . . .'

He finishes his wine and pours himself out some more. I'm still sipping mine. I can't drink it down like pop. I know I'm supposed to relate what he's just said to my own life now, but it's not easy to know where to start. 'Do you mean that Mum wouldn't have wanted me to have my hair done like this?' I ask him.

He drinks some more of the wine and thinks for a moment. 'She always used to cut your hair,' he says thoughtfully, 'and you've never asked to have it done any differently. You always wore your hair just like hers – just straight and plain. You dress the way she did. She never used to wear any make-up; you hardly ever do. She never smoked; I bet you never will . . .'

'But there's nothing wrong with that,' I interrupt him. 'You wouldn't want me to do any of those things . . .'

'No,' he says. 'But what I mean is that however you . . . however *we* choose to live . . . it's got to be because of what *we* want. Whatever *we* decide. Not because we imagine your mother standing over us still, approving or disapproving . . .' He shakes his head and smiles gently. 'And she used to disapprove of such an awful lot . . .' He turns and looks straight at me as though this is a kind of private joke for us to share between the two of us.

I smile back. It's very true. My mother was always finding things to complain about – signing petitions and writing to M.P.s – everything from selling war toys in Woolworth's to importing crocodile-skin handbags. She cared about everything, my mum.

Whilst we're on the subject, I decide to take the opportunity I've been waiting for. 'It wasn't such a bad thing that she disapproved about you drinking . . .' I tell him.

He sits for a moment, thinking, and then shakes his head again. 'No,' he answers. 'It wasn't.' He looks around at the posters on the walls advertising bullfights and foreign holiday resorts as if he wants to avoid looking straight at me. 'I used to drink a lot before I met her,' he goes on, 'but she persuaded me to give up before we got married. I just never went in a pub then . . .'

I take a deep breath and summon my strength together. 'You *can* be persuaded then,' I say, smiling, laying on the charm. It's not like me this, at all. 'You could give up, if you really wanted to.'

The waiter arrives with the pizza and the lasagne. It looks gorgeous. I sit there for a few seconds, just sniffing it.

My father puts his empty glass down on the table and

reaches for his knife and fork. He puckers up his lips and half smiles to himself. 'Well,' he says, 'I suppose I *could* . . . if I really wanted to . . .'

I decide not to go on about it. I've said what I think, and if I keep nagging him about it, it might just put him off. I pick up my cutlery and taste the lasagne. It's delicious. Really gorgeous. It must be ages since the last time I had anything really nice to eat. I take another drink of wine and watch my father cutting into the edge of his pizza. 'I've decided I want to be a Quaker,' I tell him.

I expect him to look shocked but he doesn't. He starts cutting little triangles into the melted cheese and olives with his knife. 'O.K.,' he says, as though he always knew I'd say that to him one day. 'That's fine. I'm pleased about it. Be all the good things your mother was.' He puts his knife and fork down and looks up at me. His eyes are deep blue and deadly serious. 'But copy them because they're good; not because you're afraid of standing up on your own.' He pours himself the rest of the wine and swills it round his glass. 'Be true to yourself, Rebecca,' he tells me, swallowing the wine in one gulp. 'To thine own self be true.'

22

'This speech of yours hath mov'd me,
And shall perchance do good; but speak you on;
You look as you had something more to say.'
(Edmund, Act V, Scene III)

It's Tuesday before I finally have enough courage to knock on the door of Miss Hoggit's office. I wait for one of the notices to light up. I'm feeling scared. I'm also feeling determined to go through with this scene, no matter how painful it turns out to be, but I'm feeling scared as well.

The ENTER notice lights up and I walk into the office. It brings back painful memories – worse than walking into a dentist's. 'Hello,' says Miss Hoggit, trying to look as if she's pleased to see me. 'Come in . . . Rebecca.' She isn't sure whether it's me or not at first. She keeps staring at my hair as if it's a dead hedgehog. 'Sit down.'

I close the door quietly behind me and try to keep calm and composed as I go and sit in the chair which faces Miss Hoggit's desk.

'Well?' she asks, trying hard to smile at me but not quite managing it. 'What can I do for you?'

I close my eyes for a fraction of a second and take a deep breath. 'I've come to apologize,' I say, clasping my hands together tightly on my lap. 'I'm sorry . . . that I swore at you.'

There's a silence. Miss Hoggit cringes visibly as though the memory's still painful. She doesn't say anything.

'I'm sorry I lost my temper,' I add, hoping that that's all I need to say.

'Yes,' Miss Hoggit swallows hard. She speaks very slowly and her voice is harsh. 'I intended taking further action about it, Rebecca, but . . . obviously you were very upset.'

I'm not enjoying this scene at all. Miss Hoggit isn't giving anything away; she's sitting tight-lipped and straight-faced, tapping her fancy pen on her desk. I wish I'd not come now.

'I had obviously said something that upset you,' she goes on. 'I was never able to understand what it was . . .'

She's expecting me to explain now why I lost my temper and this is something that I haven't bargained for. I've rehearsed the first bit of the conversation and the last bit, but this part in between is something I hadn't been expecting. I don't know how to explain.

The silence carries on and I feel as though I have to say something. I don't know where to start. 'I . . . I was very upset when my mother died,' I try.

'Yes . . .' Miss Hoggit says without letting up at all . . . 'but that was a long time ago now, Rebecca . . .' Another pause.

'I know.' You see, I know exactly why I got so upset, but I just can't put it into words. I don't think it's fair of her to try and make me. I squirm and look around the room. I want to change the subject.

Still Miss Hoggit waits. Her eyes stare at me, penetrating, and she continues to slide her fingers rhythmically up and down the pen in her hand. The silence deepens. The air seems heavy with tension.

In the end I realize that she isn't going to give in. I start to think about what it is she's asking me and I try to make the words form in my head. I know it's got something to do with the fact that when anybody gets at me they seem to be getting at my mother as well. That isn't easy to explain. 'My father says I've got to be myself,' I say at last.

She nods approvingly. 'And why does he say that, Rebecca?'

I go back to the evening in the restaurant: my father

holding his wine glass and swilling the wine around gently. I see him smiling at me, his blue eyes heavy with thought. I know exactly what he means. It just hurts me to think about it. 'He says that my mother had a very strong personality . . .'

I look up at Miss Hoggit and she nods her head again. I listen consciously to the Silence for a few moments.

'. . . and she did.' I pause and swallow hard. 'I've always wanted to copy her . . . the good things about her . . . and the bad ones as well . . . I haven't done things on my own.' I take a deep breath and try to get it over with quickly. 'I judge other people by what my mother used to be like . . . I judge my father . . . I judge myself . . .'

Miss Hoggit nods again but this time her look is one of sympathy. She looks at me as though she understands and the silence which follows is one of acceptance; she is accepting what I have said and waits for me to accept the fact that I've said it.

'Miss Gloucester said I ought to go to France,' I say at last. 'She thought it would be good for me. She said the school might pay for me to go . . .'

Miss Hoggit looks pleased at last. She actually smiles, but still the interrogation's not over with. 'What do you think?' she asks me. 'Do you want to go to France? Do *you* think it would be good for you?'

I stop and think. As I've said before, I believe very strongly in telling the truth so I don't always say the first thing that comes into my head. I don't always say things just to please people or because they sound right. (Come to think of it, you might have noticed this by now.) France itself doesn't particularly appeal to me, so that's not the reason I want to go. I just feel as though Miss Gloucester might be right. I need time to get away and time to be on my own. And I'd like to spend some time just fooling about with the other kids. 'Yes,' I say. 'I want to go. I think it would do me good.'

Miss Hoggit looks genuinely happy. 'I'm very pleased, Rebecca,' she says. 'Very pleased indeed. And very glad that you've come to ask me.'

I stand up, hoping to go.

'There'll be no problems about the money,' she goes on, leaning right over at me and lowering her voice. 'No problems at all. And, of course, I won't mention about it to anyone else. There's no need for anyone else to know, Rebecca, is there?' she says, trying to sound nice.

'No.'

'And', she smiles down at me as if I'm six years old again, 'we'll say no more about the other incident, Rebecca.'

'Thank you.' I try to look really grateful. I could never bring myself to like Miss Hoggit but I think perhaps she can't help being so weird. She might be struggling her hardest to be normal; you never know. 'Thank you very much,' I say, and I turn and walk out into the corridor.

23

'And drive toward Dover, friend, where thou shalt meet
Both welcome and protection.'

(Gloucester, Act III, Scene VI)

I decide to ask my dad about going to France when I've come back from taking the papers round. I walk into the kitchen and he isn't there, but he's eaten his tea and the washing-up's all done and standing in the drying rack. I go upstairs.

I have to walk past his bedroom to get to mine. As I walk across the landing, his door is open and I can see him inside the bedroom, sitting at the dressing-table. I hesitate. I want to talk to him straightaway about this trip to France whilst I can still remember what I've decided to say but he looks as though he's busy. I stand in the doorway.

He's sitting on the stool at the dressing-table that used to be my mother's and, open in front of him, is a wooden box crammed full with letters and photographs. In his left hand he's holding one of the photographs and in his right hand the crumpled page of an old letter. He's reading, deep in thought, concentrating.

I walk inside the room and stand behind him. I can see the photograph clearly now. It's a picture of my mother taken when she was young, when my father had only just met her. She looks very pretty and her eyes are bright and smiling. She has a hair band to keep the hair back from her eyes and her forehead is high and smooth without any of the wrinkles in it. She looks nice.

My father has heard me walk inside the room but he doesn't look up until he's read down to the bottom of the letter. Then he sighs deeply and stares at his reflection in the mirror. He looks sad. Very old and very sad.

'I ought to throw them away,' he murmurs, looking towards the wooden box, then he pauses . . . 'I still like to read them . . .' he says, almost as if he's apologizing to me. 'I still like to look at her handwriting . . .'

For a tiny fraction of a second it comes home to me again, the way it did when I was in the Meeting House, him, hiding away up here, absorbed in all these memories. I feel the fingers poking at my nerves again and, just for a moment, I feel his grief. When my mother died, you see, I was so upset myself – so engrossed in what effect it had on me – that I never thought about how sad my father was. No, that's not what I mean. I knew that he was sad, but I couldn't feel it. Couldn't share . . . it's not easy to explain. The nearest thing, I think, is when you're acting – when you get inside another person's head and look at everything through their eyes – then you know what it feels like to be them. The way I found out what it was like to be the people in *King Lear*. Now I'm beginning to learn, very slowly, what it's like to be my father.

Again I feel the metal fingers probe and touch me, telling me to comfort him. Telling me to touch him and again I shrink back, clumsy and afraid. Shy and embarrassed. Then I think about the Meeting – about the stranger who came up to me and patted my hand. The stranger who comforted me.

I lift my hand up as if it's made of lead. Very slowly, forcing it upwards until it reaches his right shoulder. The distance seems immense. Gently, I let the tips of my fingers rest on the soft sleeve of his jumper and then I hold them there for a moment, gingerly. 'Don't throw anything away,' I tell him, as though I'm asking him a favour.

He looks at me in the mirror with his face all sad and

worried. Then he reaches up with his left hand, moves it across to his shoulder, and searches for my fingers. For half a second just our fingertips touch. Then he reaches further up and wraps his hand, large and strong, around mine. He squeezes and pats my hand gently.

I look down at his reflection in the mirror and smile, weakly. For a moment or two our eyes meet and then he smiles at me gently. We don't say anything but I feel a kind of satisfaction. As if I've taken a step forward.

I wait until he comes downstairs before I ask about the holiday in France. Amazingly enough, he seems pleased. He says how brave it was of me to ask Miss Hoggit if the school would pay for me to go and even says that, if I'd asked him about it, he would have come up to school to talk to her himself. I don't need to say any of the things I've been rehearsing in my mind because it's all right. He wants me to go anyway. He says he'll cook all his meals himself and do the washing and ironing. He says it'll do me good to have a rest. I can hardly believe it.

At the week-end he takes me into town and buys me some clothes ready for the holiday: a zip-up jacket, two pairs of jeans, a shirt and some trainers. I've never had so many clothes at once. He hasn't got enough money to pay for them all, of course, and we have to open a thing called a budget account. It's like we have at Horace Oglet's except that the people in the shop don't look so fed up about it as he does and they give us a little card for my dad to sign.

Then he buys me a French phrase book that's full of really useful things like: 'Where can I buy an adjustable spanner?' and 'My wife would like an elastic bandage for her knee.' With a book like that I can't go wrong.

I start to look forward to the holiday.

I'm not going to go into a lot of detail about my holiday in

France because that isn't what this book's about. This book is really about what happened before I went to France, but there are just a few more things I want to finish telling you before I stop writing.

First of all, my father was a big help in getting me organized for the holiday. He helped me to pack my suitcase and kept asking if I'd got everything I needed, and he even came down to the station to see me off. It was nice. I almost felt proud of him. As you might guess, Bernice Berkshire came over with some feeble excuse about asking me if I'd got any travel sickness pills because she'd forgotten hers. She looked at my dad in a dreamy, helpless sort of way and said, 'Oooh, I am hopeless you know. I think I'd forget my own head if it was loose,' and then giggled in this ridiculously artificial sort of way she's got when she's trying too hard to make an impression. I can read Bernice Berkshire like a book. I bet she's never been travel sick in her life.

Dad was all charm and chat but didn't exactly seem over-enthusiastic about Bernice. He went and had a word with some of the other kids and parents as well and sounded amazingly normal. He wasn't drunk either.

24

'Thou hast spoken right, 'tis true.
The wheel is come full circle.'
(Edmund, Act V, Scene III)

FRANCE,
MONDAY

Dear Dad,

I'm having a great time in France and everything is going fine. It was raining when we arrived but today has been nice and sunny.

The journey here was a bit long and boring and most of us fell asleep but coming across the Channel was O.K. because you could walk about. Our French teacher was ever so seasick so we never really saw her except when she came staggering out of her cabin looking green and rolling her eyes at us (rather like you - - - after a bad night!)

The amazing thing about France is that it's ever so French. They really do sell strings of onions and have shutters on the windows and cafes where you sit on the pavement. They have some funny toilets as well.

I hope you are surviving without my cooking and give my love to Scruffbag if he's home.

Love

Rebecca

France, Tuesday

Dear Miss Gloucester,

We are all having a great time here in France and I want to say thank you for your idea about me coming. If you look on the back of this p.card you will see the castle where we went yesterday. Timothy Trotter leaned out of the window right at the top of the Tower (marked with an *) and his bobble hat flew off and landed in the fish pond.

Miss Runt got really mad when he paddled in the pond to fetch it back afterwards. Otherwise, we've all been very well-behaved and respectable (cough! cough!).

I hope you are feeling a little bit better now after your operation and will be back at school again before long. We have all missed the Drama Workshop.

How's the palm tree coming on?

Love

Rebecca O'Leary

Home.

Dear Rebecca,

Many thanks for your letter and I'm very pleased that you seem to be enjoying yourself.

I have survived amazingly well so far without your cooking although there is an enormous pile of washing-up awaiting you when you get back.

Seriously though, I have been very energetic. I have been to the launderette and hoovered the living-room and I nearly cleaned the bath on Saturday, but decided against it.

This is big news: on Saturday night, instead of

going to the pub I started wall-papering the living-room. On Sunday, instead of going to the pub, I carried on wall-papering the living-room.

On Monday night I was exhausted and watched the tele. How about that? It's not brilliant, but it's a start, isn't it? And you do realize that wall-papering can be very clinsty work?

I had a letter this morning from your drama teacher, Miss Gloucester. She said she'd had a postcard from you and hoped I didn't mind her idea about you going to France and that I was managing all right without you.

I don't know what she's

been hearing about me but she said how much she admired my "fortitude" and how she thought I must have been a "real pillar of strength to you over the past twelve months".

What have you been telling her about me?

None of it's true, anyway.

I thought about sending her a few books when I write back - not Shakespeare, exactly, but something to cheer her up a bit.

Scruffbag disappeared for three days but came back home this morning. I think he wonders where you are. Go easy on the frog's legs.

Love, Dad.

FRANCE

Dear Dad,

Thank you very much for the letter. It was nice to hear from you.

I didn't write back straightaway because I've been busy. We've been looking round lots of museums and castles and things and I've met a French boy called François who took me out to the pictures on Friday night. He's very nice but it's nothing serious. A pity the film was all in French, because I couldn't follow it. Bernice Berkshire came as well (she's the girl you met at the station) and François' friend, and they bought us some French chocolate.

The dictionary you bought me has been really useful. I've learned a lot of words they don't teach us in the French lessons and I've managed to go in the shops and make them understand what I want.

I'm very pleased about the decorating and your other "good news". How long do you think it will last? Perhaps you'd better start wall-papering the rest of the house if it helps. They drink red wine here with meals but I don't like it much.

No, I never said anything to Miss Gloucester about you so I don't know how she got the idea about you being a "pillar of strength". Perhaps she thought that anybody who put up with me would have to have some miracle ingredients.

Anyway, she's very nice. You could always <u>take</u> the books round, couldn't you? She doesn't seem to get many visitors. And whilst you're there you could give us a progress report on the palm tree we bought her.

I'll be arriving home on Sunday. The boat docks at six o'clock in the morning, if you feel like coming down to meet me (don't panic – I'm only joking).

I was going to buy you a bottle of wine as a coming-home present but I've changed my mind. I'll get you something else instead. How about a paint-roller? Or some wall-paper paste?

Love
Rebecca

I enjoyed the holiday very much, but the thing I expect you'll be most interested in is this fantastic French boy I met. His name was François and he was gorgeous. I'm not much good at describing people, but I'll try and tell you about him because just thinking about what he looked like turns me on. He was very foreign-looking; he had this dark complexion and lovely black wavy hair – not too long and always nicely washed. And he had really deep brown eyes. I saw a film star once with eyes like that but I can't remember his name. He was fairly tall and slim (I'm telling you about François now, by the way, not the film star) and he was nearly seventeen. He wore this little gold ear-ring in his left ear and he used to wear an old flying-jacket (one of those brown leather ones with a big fur collar like they had in the War) most of the time. And corduroy jeans – very tight around the legs and the . . . like I say, he was quite fantastic. I've never learned so much French in all my life as I did in those three weeks. I even learned the French for . . .

Well, as I mentioned before, this book isn't the right place to be telling you all about that. It's not supposed to be about what happened when I went to France. It's mainly about what happened before then. It's about the worst period in my life when I got really low and depressed and I thought nothing would ever turn out right for me.

When I was twelve, somebody bought me one of those little Birthday Books that have a sort of motto next to every day of the year and next to my birthday, June the twenty-seventh, it said, 'Remember that the World is a Wheel and it always comes round all right.' I didn't believe it at first but, do you know, it's true. Things do get better. They don't get fantastic all at once and sometimes you have to push them along a little bit because sitting around like a clockwork money-box, waiting for other people to come along and wind you up, is not what life is all about. I'm not going to give you a long sermon here on what life *is* all about because I don't pretend to know yet. I'm still finding out. But at least I think I'm learning.

The final thing I want to tell you about is when I came

home from France. I was very upset about leaving François because I'd only been going out with him for twelve and a half days, but he promised he'd write to me and we talked about seeing each other again next year. I don't know how we would organize that or whether we'd still want to see each other by that time but, anyway, that's what we said.

We had quite a rave up on the boat coming back from France. I wasn't the only one who'd met somebody nice on holiday, and to stop ourselves from feeling depressed and weepy, we had a big party. We all got sloshed because the French waiters in the bar never bother asking you how old you are. Gertie Runt was in bed being seasick, by the way, whilst all this was going on. Anyway, we all had plenty to drink, what with all the bottles of wine and champagne people had bought to take back with them for presents. We sat around singing in the bar with our arms round each other, and Bernice even sat on Timothy Trotter's knee for five minutes. He was in his element. I thought it was really nice of her. Then she just gave him a little peck on his cheek and went off to chat up one of the French waiters. That wasn't particularly difficult . . .

Anyway, I'm getting off the subject again because what I wanted to tell you about was arriving back in Dover. It was very early in the morning – a beautiful, clear morning in early summer and the sea was calm at last. The seagulls were swooping round in circles like seagulls are supposed to do and, although I'd expected to be really disappointed about coming home again, I actually found it very moving. When I saw the white cliffs of Dover looming up in front of us, I thought of all the thousands of English people sailing back from France over the centuries, all feeling tremendously excited to see the cliffs and know that they were home.

So, there I was, standing on the deck watching England

coming nearer and feeling very moved by it all. Then I went down to fetch my bag and waited in a big crush with the others by the doorway to the ramp ready to set off down the gangplank.

Like I say, the sun was shining; it was a beautiful day. The sea was a lovely deep blue and the cliffs were dazzling white the way they are in holiday postcards. Already I had this strange mixture of emotions swirling round inside me as I walked down the plank and looked down at all the people and I thought to myself, 'Well, this is it; this is England.' And then I saw my father.

He was standing near the front of the crowd, watching. He'd seen me already and when I looked at him, he smiled and waved. He looked different at first. He'd grown a beard – all black and bushy. It made him look a bit older somehow. He looked . . . I don't know . . . more like a father. When I actually saw him, I felt this strange mixture of emotions swirling round inside me but the amazing thing was that I was happy. When I wrote to tell him what time the boat was coming in, I never thought for a moment that he'd actually come down and meet me and, when I saw him, I was quite shocked at how I felt. I was actually pleased to see him.

I lost sight of him for a moment or two because there were all these people crowding round, waiting to get through the Customs, and I had to stand in a squash and wait my turn. But then, when I got clear, there he was still, waiting for me. I hadn't intended to hug or kiss him or anything like that, but when I came through the gate, there he was with his arms stretched out and it seemed as natural as breathing for me to just walk over and put my arms around him and hug him.

It was strange. There were things about him that I'd forgotten about because it was such a long time since we'd been so close – things that were so familiar like the smell of him, the feel of the warm leather of his jacket, the smell of his cotton shirt dampened a bit with sweat – things that brought memories racing back to me of times when I was tiny and he used to pick me up and hug me. When I'd fallen down and hurt myself or when I was frightened in the dark. I'd forgotten how he used to look after me. And in the end this memory was still there all the time, sleeping away in the corner of my mind, this image of something I could count on and come back to. Something secure. In the end it was still there. My father.

So, we hugged each other, and then he pushed me away from him a few inches and lifted my head up so that he could look at me properly. And then I had this strange kind of premonition: this sort of feeling that, all of a sudden, I knew what was going to happen in the future. Somehow it seemed to me that in the end we were going to pull through. Somehow we were going to survive. I could imagine us both struggling a bit and tottering about and making fools of ourselves sometimes but, in my mind's eye, I could see us getting there in the end. Winning.

I looked at all the people thronging round the quayside and I held on to my father and I realized for the first time that both of us had been floundering on our own through something that we just weren't able to cope with by ourselves. If only we could work together we'd be stronger. We could cope with things together that were too much for us on our own. We'd been through a lot of pain and we'd been through a lot of misery and anguish but, in spite of that, we'd both been learning. Learning to survive.

'Welcome home,' my father said to me at last and he spoke as though he meant it. 'Welcome home, love,' he said. 'It's great to have you back.'

'Thanks,' I said and hugged him again. 'I'm glad to be home.'

ALSO IN

HEINEMANN NEW WINDMILLS

General Editors: Anne and Ian Serraillier

Chinua Achebe Things Fall Apart
Douglas Adams The Hitchhiker's Guide to the Galaxy
Vivien Alcock The Cuckoo Sister; The Monster Garden; The Trial of Anna Cotman; A Kind of Thief
Margaret Atwood The Handmaid's Tale
J G Ballard Empire of the Sun
Stan Barstow Joby
Nina Bawden The Witch's Daughter; A Handful of Thieves; Carrie's War; The Robbers; Devil by the Sea; Kept in the Dark; The Finding; Keeping Henry
E R Braithwaite To Sir, With Love
John Branfield The Day I Shot My Dad
F Hodgson Burnett The Secret Garden
Ray Bradbury The Golden Apples of the Sun; The Illustrated Man
Betsy Byars The Midnight Fox; Goodbye, Chicken Little; The Pinballs
Victor Canning The Runaways; Flight of the Grey Goose
John Christopher The Guardians; Empty World
Jane Leslie Conly Racso and the Rats of NIMH
Roald Dahl Danny, The Champion of the World; The Wonderful Story of Henry Sugar; George's Marvellous Medicine; The BFG; The Witches; Boy; Going Solo; Charlie and the Chocolate Factory; Matilda
Andrew Davies Conrad's War
Anita Desai The Village by the Sea
Charles Dickens A Christmas Carol; Great Expectations
Peter Dickinson The Gift; Annerton Pit; Healer
Berlie Doherty Granny was a Buffer Girl
Gerald Durrell My Family and Other Animals
J M Falkner Moonfleet
Anne Fine The Granny Project
F Scott Fitzgerald The Great Gatsby
Anne Frank The Diary of Anne Frank
Leon Garfield Six Apprentices

Adele Geras Snapshots of Paradise
Graham Greene The Third Man and The Fallen Idol; Brighton Rock
Thomas Hardy The Withered Arm and Other Wessex Tales
Rosemary Harris Zed
L P Hartley The Go-Between
Esther Hautzig The Endless Steppe
Ernest Hemingway The Old Man and the Sea; A Farewell to Arms
Nat Hentoff Does this School have Capital Punishment?
Nigel Hinton Getting Free; Buddy; Buddy's Song
Minfong Ho Rice Without Rain
Anne Holm I Am David
Janni Howker Badger on the Barge; Isaac Campion
Linda Hoy Your Friend Rebecca
Barbara Ireson (Editor) In a Class of Their Own
Jennifer Johnston Shadows on Our Skin
Toeckey Jones Go Well, Stay Well
James Joyce A Portrait of the Artist as a Young Man
Geraldine Kaye Comfort Herself; A Breath of Fresh Air
Clive King Me and My Million
Dick King-Smith The Sheep-Pig
Daniel Keyes Flowers for Algernon
Elizabeth Laird Red Sky in the Morning
D H Lawrence The Fox and The Virgin and the Gypsy; Selected Tales
Harper Lee To Kill a Mockingbird
Julius Lester Basketball Game
Ursula Le Guin A Wizard of Earthsea
C Day Lewis The Otterbury Incident
David Line Run for Your Life; Screaming High
Joan Lingard Across the Barricades; Into Exile; The Clearance; The File on Fraulein Berg
Penelope Lively The Ghost of Thomas Kempe
Jack London The Call of the Wild; White Fang
Bernard Mac Laverty Cal; The Best of Bernard Mac Laverty
Margaret Mahy The Haunting; The Catalogue of The Universe
James Vance Marshall Walkabout
Somerset Maugham The Kite and Other Stories
Michael Morpurgo Waiting for Anya; My Friend Walter

How many have you read?